T0086164

SACRED
BEING

ALYSSIA CLEMMER

SACRED BEING

iUniverse books may be ordered through booksellers or by contacting:

iUniverse
1663 Liberty Drive
Bloomington, IN 47403
www.iuniverse.com
844-349-9409

ISBN: 978-1-6632-4313-3 (sc)
ISBN: 978-1-6632-4314-0 (e)

Print information available on the last page.

iUniverse rev. date: 07/23/2022

CHAPTER 1

HARUNA

I entered a portal to get to a world where my life won't be in danger anymore. There are two bodyguards coming with me. Haru Mori, a tall light brown-haired man, and his wife Elie Mori, a five-foot seven-inch woman with short black hair, who will be acting as my mother and father while we are hiding on Earth. I am four years old and am being chased by someone who wants to use my powers to destroy my home world, Murina, at the cost of my own life.

My real mother and father explained to me about having me go into hiding on Earth with Elie and Haru as my guardians and acting as my mother and father in their stead. They also warned me the moment we landed on Earth after going through the portal, I will forget everything about Murina and my real last name, Yashamada.I will have Haru and Elie's last name while we are in hiding.

We landed in a small village called Alorrur and went to an old broken-down house so we could get to sleep out of the wind and cold. Mother asked "Do you remember anything? You should remember your powers." I said "I remember my powers. Why would I forget about them? I can't remember anything else other than my powers and you two are my mother and father." She said "Ok, I was checking if you remembered anything. Now let's get to sleep so we can work on rebuilding this house to make it our own." I said "ok," and slept next to them to keep warm.

I sat in the kitchen after I woke up, ate breakfast, washed off, and went to mother and father. They looked at me and said, "We are going to the market to get food and get to know the villagers." I nodded and followed them to the market.

We walked to our neighbor's house to introduce ourselves. We were met in their doorway before we could even knock. They immediately asked "Why did you move into that broken down house with your four-year-old daughter?" Mother said "We are planning on rebuilding that house to live in it and make it beautiful and livable again." They looked shocked and said "oh...... If you need to stay somewhere while you work on it, you are free to live with us." Mother and father smiled and said "Thanks for the offer but we can live in our house. There is still a room in it which doesn't leak. We checked after our daughter went to sleep last night." They smiled and said "well that's good. If you ever need help building, we will help." Father grabbed my hand and started walking toward the market as Mother said "we will let you know if we ever need help" and waved as she made her way to us.

We started looking at shops and restaurants within the village. While mother and father were looking for food, I was looking around for kids my age to play with but found someone who gave me an unbelievably bad feeling and I somehow recognized him. I felt a hand go around my arm and pull me toward whoever it is who grabbed me. When I turned around, I realized it is father who grabbed me and asked" Why am I getting a bad feeling about that man?" while pointing at him. As father picked me up and carried me out the market, he said "good you still have your senses. That man is extremely dangerous. You will learn about him later, right now we need to get back home before he sees us. We will try our best to protect you from that man. Promise us you will try to stay away from him." I said "I promise" and stared at the market as we rushed to the house.

We got back to the house and started to work on it. The neighbors came over an hour later without us asking for help and started helping. I would play with the neighbors' kids and came back before dark every day. A year passed and I had to get ready for school. I got enrolled and am supposed to start in the morning, so we went to the market to get paper, ink, and a brush. The moment we got to the market, I asked "is it ok if I wander around until you get the supplies?" Mother smiled and said "Sure, we will find you when we are done. Be careful." I smiled and said" Thank you I will "as I ran off to look around.

I walked around a while before bumping into a boy with short black hair and green eyes who looked about the same age as me. I said "I'm sorry, are you ok? I wasn't watching where I was going." He helped me up and said "Its ok, I'm not hurt and wasn't watching where I was going either. I am William, who

3

are you?" I said "I am Haruna. Do you want to walk around with me? I am just wandering around until my parents get the supplies I will need for school."

He said "Sure but only for a little while because I have to leave soon because I am looking for someone." I smiled and said "thanks" and walked in a circle around the market before he left. I started to walk back toward the area I last saw mother and father but found the man from a year ago. I watched him as I tried to get out of sight but realized he is looking straight at me. I immediately ran away as he ran at me.

No matter how long or far I run, he is always behind me. I ran into the nearby forest to try and lose him but became trapped when I ran into a cave only to realize it is a dead end. I turned around to look at him as he slowly walked toward me laughing demonically. I started to think I was a goner when I felt someone grab me, run past the man and out the cave, then stopped a short distance from it. I looked at who just saved me as he put me down and was shocked to see William. He is looking past me and toward the cave we were just in, so I followed his line of sight and am surprised by what I see. Mother and father are fighting the man. As I went to run to help them, William grabbed my arm to stop me and shook his head with a serious expression.

I looked toward the fight again and heard Mother yell "Stay away from Yamato! He wants to use your powers to his own personal gain!" I am glad to finally have a name to his face and yelled back with tears in my eyes "I will unless he gives me no other choice!" She yelled "good. be careful, now go and get to safety!" I yelled "Mother, Father!" as William tugged on my arm to get me to run. As I was turning around, I saw Yamato kill them and run at us. I stopped out of a mixture of sorrow and anger making William stop in the process because he was holding onto my arm and waited for him to get close. I kicked his chest then punched his head the moment he got close sending him flying backwards into the cave. I grabbed William's hand and ran to the village with tears running down my cheeks. When I looked back at William, he had a shocked look as he ran behind me.

He said "You should be safe now." I said "I should be for now but I didn't kill him so I know he will be after me again after he heals. Be safe on your way home." He said "I don't live here. I live in a village quite a good distance from here, so I will definitely be careful. You better do the same" and ran toward the market while I went home and cried myself to sleep. My neighbors came over to check on me after they heard about mother and father being killed and started to look after me. They know it is going to be a long road with me living alone in my house and constantly helped me get through my grief.

CHAPTER 2

I went through the school year passing kindergarten. I woke up in the morning and got ready for school. I went through kindergarten without making any friends because their parents think I am the cause of my parents' deaths. A year ago, when I saw William run toward the market after Yamato killed Mother and father, he was running to tell the adults of my parents' murders and about me going into hiding from the man who had killed them. They have been searching for him without any luck. They learned shortly after Yamato was originally after me, so they won't let their kids play with me because they think he is still after me and I don't blame them, I know he is still after me. It's a feeling I have, and I have learned to trust those feelings.

My neighbors aren't afraid of him and can handle themselves, so they still let their kids play with me when I am not studying or working on my house. I decided to continue living in my parents unfinished house and work on it when I can. I have a special class because I have completed the highest amount of work required for the school, I am in. I help the teachers grade the students work when I am not in my special class which is

Martial arts and higher graded work from the academy they deliver by carrier to the school. I keep the house clean and repair it when I have time. My neighbors help when I repair the house when I work on it. I always walk with their kids so they don't get hurt and so I can watch over them.

I started to walk home with my neighbors' kids but had to fight some kidnappers who are trying to kidnap one of their classmates. I knocked them out, walked her and the others to their houses, then went home and to bed after eating when I got there. I ate breakfast and went to school in the morning and noticed people whispering and pointing at me which made me wonder what is wrong all day.

WILLIAM

I watched Haruna leave her school and didn't want her to know I am watching so I stayed hidden. I noticed the kids staring at her and whispering as she left. I decided to follow her a while longer and watched as she got food and supplies for her house at the market. I would have watched over her longer if I didn't have to go back home to Romora. I waited for her to get to her house with the supplies before I went home.

HARUNA

I wondered why they continued to whisper around me all week. I went to school the following week and noticed a boy wasn't paying any mind to everyone's whispering. When he made eye contact with me, I decided to walk up to him and asked "why is everyone whispering when I walk past them?" He said "they are whispering dark things about you and keep telling everyone you are a murderer and should not trust you. They think they should do something about you before someone else dies. Don't worry I don't think you are a murderer and trust you over anyone else, so you will definitely not have a problem with me." I am a little confused with what he told me but said "Thanks" then walked away. He said "no problem" before walking away as well. I turned around and watched him go when I had a DeJa'Vu. His name came to me when I noticed a little blue cat with yellow stripes following him by his feet. I whispered "Ren" as he turned the corner.

When I got out of class, I heard a commotion not far from where I am now and followed the noise and voices. When I got to the commotion, I found a couple of the older students holding Ren by his arms while one of their friends held his cat. I ran up to them and yelled "leave Ren alone and let him go!" They looked at me while continuing what they were saying before my interruption "this is what you get for telling her what we were going to do" while smiling and tightened their grip on both Ren and his cat. I kicked one of them across the hallway the moment the last word came out of their friends mouth then punched the other one holding Ren in the face forcing them to let him go. I spun around and grabbed the cat at the same time as I kicked the last one of them into the wall. The moment he hit the wall he was unconscious, and his friends are now staring at me in complete shock and pain.

Ren looked at them than me and said "thanks but I could have handled it and how do you know my name?" as his cat jumped out of my arms and ran to him. I said "sorry I don't like when they do things like that so it doesn't matter if you could handle it or not and your name came to me shortly after I had a DeJa'Vu when we talked earlier." He looked shocked but happy at the same time and said "oh…well I got to go…. thanks sis" as he walked away. The teachers walked up to me and asked, "why did you fight those kids?" I said "I fought them because they were hurting someone. I stopped them." The students who saw what happened agreed with me and the teachers said "ok, we will take them to the nurse and punish them. That boy you helped was visiting from a dojo in a far-off village and wanted to see the child who is a master at our dojo, so he left after seeing you. He probably left because he saw how well you fought these kids" as she picked the unconscious student up. I looked in the direction Ren left and wondered why he called me sis? Do I remind him of his sister?

After any other fights I would break up, the people involved would get punished after their wounds were patched up. Three years have passed, and I still haven't had much luck making friends although I do get a lot of respect from everyone. Every time there is a fight, I break it up. My powers are growing stronger everyday even though no one knows about them. Everyone started talking about the school talent show and I decided to be in it.

I waited until my class ended before I went to the dojo to sign up. I figured it was time to reveal my powers to everyone,

everyone in the school that is. I walked up to the teachers signing people up and told them about my powers. They didn't believe me, so I controlled the water in their cups. They said "so that's how you have been knocking the students out without leaving a mark on them." I said "yes, I don't like hurting people unless I absolutely have to." They said" that's a good way to keep out of trouble" and signed me up as the final act.

I started to think of something to wear for the show and decided to stick with my school uniform which is a black and white skirt which goes down to my knees and a black top. The talent show is about to start so I walked to the teachers who directed me to a room to wait and said "wait here until we call you out."

WILLIAM

I heard Haruna's school is having a talent show and decided to go see how much talent the kids really have. I rode a horse to Alorrur two days before the show at full speed and managed to make it in time. When I got to her school, the teachers lead me to the dojo and seated me furthest from the side the students are doing their acts. I had to be accompanied by five guards because mother and father know where I went this time. The teachers let everyone know I am here and to be on their best behavior.

All the acts were over and were pathetic, so pathetic it almost put me to sleep. I was about to leave when the announcer said "now for our final act is a girl born with an ability like no other. Here is Haruna Mori." Once I saw her walk out the room and heard her name, I knew she is the same Haruna I met and helped back then. When she had everyone's attention, she started her show and controlled the water from the tubs in the corners of the room. She took the water above her head then added wind, fire, and rocks then returned the rocks and water to the tubs and stopped controlling the wind and fire making the fire disappear. When the show was over, I went home and realized her powers have grown stronger. I secretly followed her home before I left.

CHAPTER 3

I went back to the inn and sat on my futon. I can't stop thinking about Haruna and have finally realized I have fallen in love with her the first day I saw her when she bumped into me, but I also sensed her powers even though they weren't fully developed yet. I am also surprised she revealed her powers without fear of the consequences. I also have powers like hers and remember mother and father told me about a girl from another world called Murina who was chased to Earth and how we need to protect her with our lives, however they probably didn't expect me to fall in love with her.

I keep trying to think of ways to get her to mother and father and after a couple hours finally decided on two options. I looked at my two most trusted guards, Yuki, a tall brown-haired boy with green eyes and Kagome, a tall girl with black waist length hair with light blue eyes and said "I have a very important and special mission for you two. I need you two to give Haruna this invitation to the castle and to watch over her until I get back to her." They took the invitation and said "yes milord, but it might take a while for us to find her to give it to *her....... it might take a few years. You have seen how fast she moves through the streets."*

I said "I know however I need you to stay here and do the mission I have given you. If you can't give her the invitation, protect her when you find her. I'll explain why you two didn't come back with me to father. I'll see you two later and good luck on finding her. I am leaving in the morning so get a good night of sleep." They said "yes milord" and went to sleep.

HARUNA

I ate breakfast in the morning and walked to mother and fathers' graves which are in the neighboring village called Burruna. I packed a small lunch and water than started the long walk to the graveyard.

YUKI

Kagome and I woke up in the morning and got ready to search for Haruna. We packed a bag with some food and water. Prince William woke up, got ready, and said "good luck on finding her. Here is some money for food and water should you need it. Be careful and do what you think will be best." I said "thank you, Kagome and I will get started immediately" as he left with the remaining guards.

HARUNA

I spent six hours at their graves and got tired, so I made a make-shift bed in the bushes behind their graves and fell asleep.

I still have dreams about the night they were murdered however somehow learned to endure them. I watched my surroundings as my conscious faded and I fell into a deep sleep.

YUKI

We looked for Haruna all day but didn't find her just by looking so we began asking around and were told by some kids from her school about her visitations to her parents' graves. When we asked where the graveyard is they simply said "Burruna". We said "thanks" as we walked in Burrunas direction but shortly after setting up camp so we could get some sleep.

HARUNA

I got up in the morning and looked around feeling the normal presence as I always did. I smiled and said "I will always love and miss you mother and father. I will be back to visit again soon" than started to walk home but was stopped by a tall blue-eyed woman with light brown hair in a carriage. She said "Haruna, I have been searching for you. The school dojo needs you. I am the new school headmaster." I said "alright, thanks. I'll go immediately....... How did you know I am the person you were looking for?" She said "The teacher in charge of the school dojo gave me a description to go by and a sketch just in case I forgot. Do you want me to take you to the school?" I said "if you wouldn't mind" and got onto her carriage as she nodded.

CHAPTER 4

She said "They seemed confident I would bring you to them." I said "thanks, I'll see why they are eager" and got off shortly after her carriage stopped. After I went into the training room, I noticed the students of the dojo are also here and are getting a lecture on self-defense. The teacher looked at me and said "I need to talk to Haruna for a little bit. Stay here and try to remember what you recently learned if you were paying attention" then motioned for me to follow him into a room two doors down.

He said "I'm glad Susan found you. I got permission from the others to ask you this. Would you like to be an instructor at our dojo? You are the most skilled person in the school and although you are finished with the school teachings, we think you should still go to classes like normal and help tutor the other students when needed." I said "absolutely, I wouldn't mind tutoring the others and become one of your instructors." He smiled and said "That's fantastic news. I am lecturing the new members of the dojo on the basics of self-defense and am about to dismiss them. As you already know, our dojo stays open even when the school itself is on break." I said "I know.

do the others know?" He said "yes" and headed back to the room everyone is in.

I stayed in the corner of the room and listened to his lecture. After he finished the lecture, the members looked at me then back at him and asked "Who and why is she here?" He said "she is Haruna. I'll explain when the other members arrive in a week. We are going to start the training when the schools break ends." I said "I know who all the new members are now, so I am going to go on home. I will continue to come here during the break" and left as he said "ok, you are always welcome here." I did the chores then went to sleep after eating.

YUKI

We got to the graveyard and searched for Haruna around the graves but didn't find her. We will never give up until we find her. We started going door to door that night and got little information on her whereabouts until we got to a little brown house. When we knocked on the door a tall, light brown haired, blue eyed young woman answered. We said "hello, I am Yuki, and this is Kagome. We are searching for a girl known as Haruna Mori. Do you know her?" She said "yes, she is starting to teach at the school dojo. If you want, I can take you there. I am the headmaster there." I said "no, thank you for offering though. Will you please keep our visit a secret from her?" She said "only if you are trying to protect her." We said "We are protecting her however, had to find her location first" in perfect sync. She nodded and said "than I will keep your visit from her.

We said our goodbyes and went our separate ways. Since we know where Haruna is, we started to fight criminals who got in the proximity of her as we began watching over her. We will continue to secretly watch over her instead of giving her the invitation.

HARUNA

The week went by fast, and it is finally time to start teaching in the dojo. When all the members arrived, the master of the dojo started to give the announcement. He said "everyone already knows Haruna, and the new members met her during the break. Starting today she is an instructor alongside me. I will be teaching the new members while she teaches the older members." The older members said "oh you had to find a stronger instructor didn't you" and put their heads in their hands while others looked down. The new members looked at them with confusion. The instructor laughed and said "you will understand later" and began the lessons.

The days went by fast and when I am not teaching or tutoring, I help around the office or visiting the local fire house to visit my friend Kyo and help him find ways to fire calls. I also work on my house when I have time.

CHAPTER 5

During the day, I work on the house and clean up around the outside and inside of it than go to bed. The neighbors always come over and help when they have time. I found new routes to areas where fires are frequent and within two years, I became well known around Alorrur and Burruna. When the villagers needed my help, they would ask when they knew I am in the area. After another year I decided to take a break from working at the school dojo so I can finally finish rebuilding my house and visit mother and father's graves as I always do. I decided to work on the house all day and go to mother and father's graves to stay with them for a while.

YUKI

We followed her to her house so we will know where it is before we went to report to lord William. The moment we got to his room he asked "Did you finally find her?" I said "yes milord" as Kagome sat down in a nearby chair. He said "ok I'm guessing you two are going to watch over her since you didn't bring her with you." I said "yes, we have decided to watch over her until she finishes her work with the dojo and school." He said "very well, I explained everything to mother and father. They said 'keep up the good work'." We said "yes milord" in sync then I continued "We will go back to Haruna. We will come back with her when she finishes what she is doing." He said "go ahead, be safe and protect her until next we meet" as we left the room and headed back to Alorrur. We went to her house the moment we got back to Alorrur but didn't find her, so we locked onto her energy and followed it to the graveyard in Burruna.

ELIE

Haru and I are watching over Haruna while she is asleep like we always do when she visits and have noticed two people in a tree not far from us. When we looked closer, we realized they are the two retainers who are with the family who are close friends with our masters and Haruna's parents who eventually took refuge on earth. We know they will not harm Haruna and know they see us but by the look on their faces it seems they will not come any closer. After a few hours we noticed them looking past us and turned around to find a few bandits sneaking closer toward Haruna, so we scared them to the brink of death.

YUKI

Kagome and I know Haru and Elie love her to the point where they will protect her while she is in the graveyard but know they cannot leave it, so we will look after her for both them and lord William.

HARUNA

Morning came and I went to the middle school to train their new master of their dojo before I went to the high school. I said "bye and don't worry he is as good as me so the students should not have a problem with him. I am going to start going to the high school to stay with my class" to Susan and the other teachers then went with the students for the next four years before I graduate with my class.

I was about to enter the school when I noticed everyone was waiting for me. A woman with long black hair down to her waist with crystal blue eyes walked up to me as I am walking to meet them. The woman who walked up to me whom is the principle said "Hello Haruna, we have been expecting you. My name is Katara. We know about you, Susan told us you finished academy level work in the elementary school and taught at the dojo there." I said "Nice to meet you guys too and what Susan said is true. I finished academy level work and taught at the middle school dojo."

She said "ok, you can teach at our dojo with the other dojo masters and when fights break out, you can stop them since we heard from our dojo master who took over the middle school dojo for you told us how strong you are and how well you can fight also don't worry all the teachers know who you are so you won't be mistaken for a student." I said "don't worry there won't be a lot of fights while I am at this school. I am going to start memorizing the school so I will know where everything is and start teaching at your dojo."

She said "ok, we are going to get everything set up in the classrooms while you are getting used to everything." I had the school memorized by the time the sun was high in the sky and went home then went to sleep so I could get an early start to the school day. I got to the school before everyone except Katara and together with all the teachers (when they came) prepared for anything that could happen. When the students came, I knew I am going to have a lot of fights to break up because four fights have already started, and school just started two minutes ago.

CHAPTER 6

I got to separating the fights. Everyone except the students I went to elementary school with and taught at the middle school dojo were surprised a girl of my physic stopped the fights and stayed away from me while I walked around but when some of them realized I am an instructor at the dojo, they understood why I broke up the fights. The teachers had a relaxing day while there were no fights.

A week passed and everyone seemed to be back to themselves and began fighting again. Once again, I jumped into it and stopped them. A small group of four students walked up to me and asked "Who do you think you are and why do you keep breaking up everyone's fights?" I said "You do not need to know who I am. Now get back to class and stop fighting so I won't have to keep breaking your fights up." They said "NO!! We will not get back to class and you can't make us since you are not a teacher." I said "You are wrong on both accounts....... now get back to class before you regret it."

As I turned around to go back to the dojo, I heard one of the males' whispers "Lets teach this girl a lesson about fights and show her how weak she really is" then ran at me. I waited for *him to raise his fist at me before I turned around and blocked his blow. I continued to block their blows while all four of them continued to attack me from all four directions at once. Even though I always keep my sword in the dojo while I teach, I always bring it when I break up fights but will not use it on the students, so I am continuing to block them.*

UNKNOWN

I noticed a fight between Haruna and four students, so I ran to the office to let Principle Katara know what is going on.

KATARA

A boy ran into my office and said "MA'AM!!!!! Four students are fighting Haruna!" I said "Don't worry, Haruna can handle herself and she really needed to teach these kids to get along for a while now." He said "What!? but...." "We need to get the teachers to the fight and move it to the dojo because once one of them gets a hit on her, she will take them out" I cut in before he could finish his sentence. He said "ok, we will watch her teach them a lesson because I am a student at the dojo and know what she is capable of."

I said "Now let's get the teachers to the dojo and have them separate the ones fighting Haruna from those who aren't." We got to the fight and yelled "STOP!!!!!" Haruna looked while still dodging their punches and kicks until I had everyone's attention. Once I had their attention I said "I will allow everyone who wants to fight Haruna fight however not here, so we are going to the dojo courtyard. Those who were already fighting her will continue when everyone gets situated. Everyone else will go to the sides of the courtyard to wait their turn or watch. The teachers will stand at the edge of everyone and make sure they behave. Now let's go."

CHAPTER 7

Everyone made their way to the courtyard while I stood in the middle of it with the four students whom I have been dodging while not really wanting to fight them. I continued to wait for Katara to give the go ahead to continue and will hold back while fighting them. Once she gave the go ahead, I knocked out three of them out cold in a short while: two were male and the other female. The other one is male and asked "How can you fight so well while you are still a student?" I said" I am not exactly a student. I am one of the masters at the dojo and Katara has asked me to stop any fights that break out." He had a surprised look and asked "How did a girl like you get strong enough to be a master of a dojo while still in school?" I said "Experience" and continued to dodge his blows. I finally managed to knock him out and looked at Katara.

Katara said "the next group can now come over." I sensed something bad was coming this way and yelled "I will have to fight them later. Instead of many groups fighting me, I'll just fight everyone who wants to fight me all at once, but it'll have to wait. Right now, you need to get everyone out of here now!"

I listened to the wind in the courtyard while everyone started to move and yelled "Too late! Protect the students!" after I heard and felt a change in the atmosphere. As everyone started to look at me, five assassins appeared in a circle around me. I said "You had to wait until I was in school to attack me didn't you" with anger in my voice. The leader of the group said "you are a hard girl to find Haruna. We were paid a lot of money to capture you. We will not fail our mission, even if we have to injure you." I said "So you have been hired by Yamato to capture me. Well, it was a mistake taking this job but lucky for you I don't kill unless I have to and haven't had to yet so far. I will only knock you out." He said "go ahead and try" and attacked me. Once we started to fight, I realized I would have to use my sword because they drew their weapons and started swinging at me. They managed to injure me quite a bit before I managed to knock them out.

I looked at Katara and said "now I can fight the rest of the students after we move the assassins out of the way." Katara said "but your injuries........" I said "Don't worry, I can still handle the kids. They are weaker than the assassins who just came after me." she nodded, and twenty students walked up to me. Sure, enough I didn't let them touch me and knocked them all out in a very short time, even with my injuries. Katara told the teachers to call the sheriff to pick up the assassins, but they were already gone. Instead, the teachers watched the unconscious students while Katara took care of my wounds because I refused to go to the hospital.

She said "That was amazing, you beat the assassins without using your powers and still managed to knock out twenty kids at the same time with terrible injuries." I said "thank you, I told you they were no problem and knew I could defeat them. It was easy with the kids but not the assassins." She said "I bet it was...... now let's get you patched up so you can heal." I said "ok" and let her clean me up and put bandages on.

When I came out of the nurse's office, everyone kept telling me they were amazed I was able to do what I did with such terrible injuries. I kept telling them "I always fight people and can fend them off no matter who it is...... even assassins." Although I don't know why Yamato sent assassins to capture me instead of doing it himself. The kids continued to fight even though I always break them up......... within half a year they gave up fighting and started to get along to try and stay on my good side and knew they would never beat me in a fight or get away with fighting while I am still around.

CHAPTER 8

The rest of the year passed, and summer break started. I worked on the house most of the time and helped others who were also working on their houses when they needed me. I was walking through the village to get supplies for my house when I heard yelling from the direction of the market.

I started to walk toward the screams when I was stopped by one of the girls who worked in the market. She said "Haruna, you have to get out of here! There is something attacking the market and I don't think even you can stop it." I said "what is it? I'll have to try fighting it and give everyone a chance to evacuate." She said "no, you can't! It is a mythical creature that was thought to be extinct, and it is going on a murderous rampage."

I said "I will try to deal with it." She said "go ahead and try but I am going to get out of here before I get killed." I ran to the market and was surprised to see a chimera attacking. I will probably have to use my powers for this one. I got in front of it and used fire to burn its face. It reeled back in pain and started to come at me. I then started to continuously use my sword to strike at its legs and tail.

WILLIAM

I heard noises coming from the market while I was walking to meet up with and check on Yuki and Kagome and ran toward the noises. I am surprised to see Haruna fighting a chimera. I started to think of something to help her defeat it when I remembered Mother and Father mentioned some creatures from her home planet may come here to bring her back. I immediately ran up to it when she jumped away from it and summoned a portal to send it back to Murina.

HARUNA

I was surprised to see William run in front of the chimera and make it disappear. I walked up to him and asked "What did you do to make it disappear like that and why are you here? I thought you said you don't live around here." He said "Don't worry about that right now. I am visiting the area and noticed you fighting a chimera, so I wanted to help you out." I said "thank you for helping. I'm sorry but I need to get home. It was nice to see you again." He said "you are welcome, and I will see you later. It was nice to see you too." I headed back to my house and fell asleep.

WILLIAM

I got to Yuki and Kagome and asked "Where were you when that chimera attacked?" They said "We were watching Haruna like you told us to and saw her get attacked by it." I asked "Why didn't you help her?" Yuki said "she just started fighting it not long before you came and sent it back to Murina. We were about to help her." I said "very well, good work than."

CHAPTER 9

The rest of the year passed calmly, and I managed to finish repairing and remodeling my house. It went from an old broken-down house to a luxurious mansion with a fountain in the courtyard and woods back behind it. My neighbors said "it has turned out nicely" as they walked up to me. I said "yes it did and I couldn't have done it without your help throughout the years."

I then said "I have to go to the school now so, I'll see you later." They said "ok, be careful walking there." I said "I will" and started to walk to school. When I got there, Katara walked up to me and said "since the freshmen don't know about you and your influence here, I have made an assembly for everyone. You are to go to the center of the courtyard again. The upperclassmen will go to one side of it while the freshmen will go to the other."

I said "very well, that is fine by me. It's easier to teach the lesson in the beginning rather than later." She said "that is why I am going to hold an assembly at the beginning of every year so you can teach them a lesson and everyone is already in the courtyard waiting for you." I said "ok, let's get started" and walked to the middle of the courtyard."

Katara walked in front of the freshmen and said "if you know what is good for you, you should never fight in school unless it is in the dojo and stay on Haruna's good side. Do not make her mad and she will not take drastic measures." The freshmen didn't listen to her warning and started to say "how can a girl who looks so skinny and fragile break up a fight between anyone? you are a weak little girl who needs to learn her place." The upper classmen yelled "she is stronger than she looks and is also the strongest person in both Alorrur and Burruna and you really should stay on her good side, or you will learn to regret it!"

I said "don't worry if they don't believe you guys then they can get their strongest male and female to come to the middle of the courtyard and fight me on a two on one brawl." They said "ok we will watch because it looks like they don't believe us. oh well we tried to warn them." Their strongest male walked toward me with a girl I'm guessing is their strongest female right beside him and said "shut up! We will teach this girl her place." Katara said "they tried to warn you how strong she is. Haruna, go easy on them please." I said "always do" as they lunged at me at the same time while my attention was still on Katara. I said "if that is how you are going to fight, I won't hold back" while dodging them then I jumped behind and hit them on the back of their necks knocking them out cold. There were not that many fights to break up after the assembly and it let me teach in the dojo more often.

32

YUKI AND KAGOME

We watched Haruna from a nearby tree and thought to ourselves 'two more years before prince William will reunite with Haruna but until then we will continue to watch over her while he is away on important business with his mother and father in the palace.'

CHAPTER 10

We would visit Haruna's mansion to keep an eye on her while she was home but once she left, we would continue to follow and watch over her and once she went to school, we would climb a nearby tree or bush and watch her from a distance.

HARUNA

I woke up in the morning for the last day of school and went to the office to get started on helping the teachers with troublesome students. When I went to teach at the dojo, Katara came and asked me for help with them. That morning I stayed on my guard because I had a very bad feeling I couldn't shake.

I told Katara about it and she said "try to ignore it since it is the last day of school. I don't think anything will happen and I can't stop classes just to investigate." I said "Katara, you know I can't ignore it. I have learned to trust these feelings when I get them. I will just stay on guard all day and keep an eye on the students."

One of the teachers called for me and said to come immediately. As I was walking to her classroom, she stopped me in the hall and said "one of my students brought someone to school who is not supposed to be here. Can you help me tell him his friend can't be in here since he is not a student."

I said "ok, I will help you and have a talk with this boy and get his friend out of the school." She said "ok, I will go to the front of the classroom and wait for you to get him out." I nodded and walked into the room. As soon as I walked in, the boys friend said "I have been searching for you Haruna" with an evil smirk. I said "everyone, get out of here. This boy wants me, and I don't want anyone to get hurt on my account. Rema, go to Katara and tell her I will be a while so have the other instructors in the dojo while I am handling this."

They said "ok" and went out of the room. Once they left the boy said "I had to come to this ridiculous school to find you because this is the only place I could find information on you." He sighed and continued "You are a hard girl to find in this world. I heard stories about you helping this school, so I brainwashed one of the students who go to this school and made them bring me here."

I said "I knew you weren't normal the moment I saw you, so I had everyone leave. Now tell me why you are after me." He said "because you are the princess of Murina and was sent away to earth for your protection, but they don't understand you are still in danger and had better come with me now. If you don't, I will set the school on fire and the ones hold dear will get hurt." I said "No, I won't go with you and will not let you harm anyone in this school." As I turned around and was about to reach the door, a wall of fire hit me and just *before I passed out heard him yell "YOU WON'T SAVE THEM IN TIME!!"*

REN

I protected my sister from the bulk of the fire, but her arm still got burnt. I will continue to protect her from Yamato until she remembers me and everything about herself and Murina. For the time being I must go somewhere else, but I will always know when she is in danger because I am her twin brother and have a special connection with her.

CHAPTER 11

YUKI

As I was about to switch trees with Kagome, I noticed some of the students and teachers running toward the office in a panic. I looked at Kagome as she jumped out the tree and started running toward the school. I yelled to her remembering she has inhuman hearing "What is wrong? Why is everyone in a panic?!" As she was about to reply, we heard the students yell "the building is on fire! Run!!!" Everyone started running for the doors and saw us running toward them.

We saw Katara run toward us, so we stopped and asked "What is going on here?" She said "Haruna was sent to investigate someone who was having trouble with an unwelcome intruder. She told Rema and her students to leave the classroom so she could have a word in private with the student's friend and not long after there was an explosion. When Rema opened the classroom door to see what it was, flames shot out and she ran to us and sounded the alarm."

We asked 'What about Haruna?" She said "she is still in the room." We are going in after her." She said "no, as much as

I want to let you go and go myself, we can't. I trust her. She will get herself out. She is strong and unique." We said "ok, we will wait for her here and we know about her powers, that is why we are watching over her and one more reason, but we cannot say it."

HARUNA

I woke up to a sharp pain on my arm and the heat of the room being ingulfed in flames. I stopped the pain by putting water around the burns on my arm. The blast from the fire wall must have knocked me unconscious because when I looked around the boy was gone, and everything is on fire. I threw water in the doorway to put it out and see how bad the fire is. It had spread to six rooms on either side of the room I am in. There was no way out, so I ran to a window and smashed it open then jumped out. It was a two story drop and when I landed, Katara ran up to me and asked "are you ok? I was worried about you because you were in the room when the explosion went off. What happened in there?"

I said "I will explain later, right now we need to go get Kyo and the rest of his men here to help put out the fire. It has spread to twelve other rooms." Katara said "ok, I will go get them." I said "alright, I will go to the others and see if everyone is accounted for" and started walking to everyone when I heard a scream and saw Rema running toward me. She yelled "FUMI AND ASAMI ARE MISSING!!!!! They aren't with the other students!"

I yelled back "I will go and find them! stay with the students!!"
I ran to Katara and said "Fumi and Asami are missing. I am
going to do a scan of the area to find them." She nodded and stood
next to me. I started my scan and found them. Katara saw the
worry in my eyes and said "they are in the school aren't they?" I
said "yes, I am going in after them. Bring everyone to the front
of the school so nothing bad will happen to them." She said "ok"
and started to get everyone together. As I started to run to the
school two people ran up beside me. I asked "who are you and
why are you coming with me?" They said "I am Yuki, and she is
Kagome. We want to help you. We are going with you." I said
"ok, just be careful." They said "we will" and ran in with me.

KAGOME

We went where Haruna was running to and found a boy
holding two kids while the room they are in is on fire. The boy
said "I told you, you would not be able to save everyone in time.
These two will not survive now." Haruna said "I won't let you
kill them. I will get them back before you can do them anymore
harm." The boy said "just try and see" and started to walk away
with them then turned around and said "oh...... and my name
is Jiro." Haruna rushed at him, grabbed Fumi and Asami, then
yelled "NOW!!!!! Attack him while you two have a chance!"

HARUNA

I watched as they darted at Jiro and brought him to the
ground. I was about to walk to him and force him to answer

39

some questions, but he disappeared out from under them. I said "I will find him later. Right now, we need to get them out of here." They nodded and started to follow me while carrying Fumi and Asami to paramedics. They wanted to treat me too, but I said "in a little bit" because I saw William walking toward me with three other people. I asked Yuki and Kagome to stay with Fumi and Asami and started to run toward him.

WILLIAM

I yelled "HARUNA!!! STOP, there is someone coming behind you!" She stopped and looked behind her. As my three guards and I started to run for her, a boy appeared in front of her and shocked her until she passed out. I hurried to her as he started to pick her up. My guards knocked her out of his hands and started to attack him. I caught her before she hit the ground. The boy was captured, and I told my guards "I am going to stay here with Yuki and Kagome to watch over Haruna. You three take the boy back to the castle and put him in the dungeon until I say otherwise and chain him to the cell wall." They said "yes my lord" and went back to the castle.

HARUNA

I woke to William carrying me to the paramedics and Katara. I asked "William? Why are you here and why are you carrying me?" He said "I heard your school was on fire and a boy started it. Once I saw the boy attack you, I knew he is the one who did it. I will find out if he works for Yamato and

I am carrying you because with the number of volts he sent through you I know you will not be able to walk on your own for a short while. I am taking you to the paramedics so they can patch you up." I said "ok," and let him carry me to them. Katara walked over and asked "are you ok?" I said "yes, I am going to help the firemen put out the fire after they patch me up and am able to walk again." She said "ok, let's hope you and the firemen remain safe while you put out the rest of the fire." I said "we will" and finished getting patched up and was able to move a few moments later.

CHAPTER 12

I walked to Kyo and said "I am going to help put out the fire." He said "I know how you are since you helped us find ways to get to our calls. You are always welcome to help whenever you want." I said "exactly, I am going to the edge of the school and start putting the fire out there." He said "ok, be careful." I said "I will, You guys had better be careful as well" and started to control water from the particles in the air to start to slowly put the fire out.

After I finished helping Kyo and his men, I went to check on Fumi and Asami who ended up being just fine. They ended up passing out from the smoke after Jiro grabbed them. After the incident with Jiro no one fought other than at the dojo because they understand why Katara let me take control around here. It is because I care deeply for anyone who steps foot in the school and will protect them. I started to walk home when someone yelled "Haruna, there are bandits terrorizing the inn and they have hostages!!!" I said "thanks for telling me, I'll be right there" and ran to the inn. The guards were already there."

42

WILLIAM

We ran to the inn as fast as we could knowing it is staged and Haruna will be there. I yelled "I should have taken him to the palace myself so we wouldn't be in this mess right now!" Yuki said "It isn't your fault. The guards you sent with him underestimated him. There is no mistaking it now, he definitely works for Yamato." I yelled "Yea and we have to get to Haruna before he does!"

HARUNA

I ran to the guard holding everyone back and asked "can I help you with anything?" He said "no, now get back and let us handle it." I said "sorry, but I can't do that. Not when hostages are involved" then ran to the front of the inn. The guard yelled "No don't!!! It is too dangerous Haruna!" I said "It is a risk I am willing to take" then rushed in before he could stop me.

CHAPTER 13

WILLIAM

We got to the inn right as Haruna went inside. I told Yuki and Kagome to stay with the guards and help them hold everyone back while I went in after Haruna.

HARUNA

I went through passages to the back of it to free the hostages. I found them and started to lead them out but was grabbed from behind. Suddenly all the hostages stood up with daggers in their hands pointing them at me. I asked "What is going on? Weren't you just being held captive?"

Jiro walked into the room and said "Haruna, you really don't remember anything about Murina do you? This is good for us because we will force you to destroy it for us whether you want to or not." I said "I will never destroy any world for you. I will always protect them and what were you talking about, me being the princess of Murina earlier?" The imposters gasped as if he didn't tell them anything. He said "yes Haruna, you are the princess of Murina, and your powers alone can destroy or heal Murina as you see fit." I looked at Jiro as if he was insane because why would I be in this world if I am the princess of another? He said "now it is time for you to sleep" and lunged at me.

WILLIAM

I ran and blocked his blow before he could hit her. I said "trying to force her over to your side was a bad idea because now you have me to deal with." I grabbed Haruna and manipulated the wind to knock them out. When we walked out after tying everyone, we told the guards "We tied them up for you. All you have to do now is get them." Haruna asked while looking me in the eyes "Why does Jiro keep saying I am the princess of Murina?" I answered "because you are, and people have been after you since even before the day you first arrived. You will learn when the rest when the time is right."

She looked at me and said "ok, well I need to get home, so I'll see you later." I said "see you later" and met up with Yuki and Kagome. We followed her to her house and decided to sleep in the woods behind it so we could be close to her.

CHAPTER 14

HARUNA

I continued to teach the students my senior year knowing people like Jiro are still after me. Katara noticed I am getting distracted more and tried not to let me work as much as I usually do but I still did even though she wanted me to take it easy. I just couldn't get the fact of me being a princess out of my head. I started to check on everyone when Katara stopped and told me to get to the courtyard because she forgot to do the assembly at the start of the year, and we are already two weeks into the school year.

I said "ok" and walked to the center of the courtyard. A few moments later Katara got everyone together. She said "standing in the center here is Haruna Mori and she is going to show you what happens when you fight and do not listen while you are here. Now if Yuri and Kurama will please come over to the center too." Katara walked up to me and said "I almost forgot, William and two of his friends came to watch you show them the ropes."

I said "ok, thank you for letting me know." She nodded while saying "you're welcome" then turned around and continued "Yuri and Kurama are who the freshmen thinks are the strongest people in the school while everyone else knows they are not. We are going to show you who truly is the strongest in the school. These three are going to fight in a two on one match. Now let it begin and don't hold anything back."

We started fighting and the freshmen yelled "She is so dead!" while the others said "no she's not" and started to out cheer them. Sometime later I knocked them out. Just as I was about to talk to the freshmen, I heard a change in the wind and yelled "KATARA, GET BACK!" and looked toward the doorway to the courtyard while getting into a defensive position. Yuki and Kagome rushed to grab Yuri and Kurama then rushed to the freshmen and put a barrier up around them. William did the same with the others just as lightning hit me. I deflected it with my sword and shoved it into the ground at my feet then yelled "You have some nerve shooting lightning at me!"

The girl standing in front of me said "you will pay for catching Jiro" and shot fire at me. I immediately swirled my arms in a circular motion and extinguished the fire with the motion of the wind I had made leaving only sparks behind. I then yelled "William! Can you still attack while maintaining the barrier?" He said "yes" while I shot lightning back (which I had trapped in my sword) at her. He grabbed her and made vines grow around her body making her fall to the ground with a grunt.

CHAPTER 15

I asked William to take her to the holding cells with the guards watching her while I went to talk to Katara and let the student's study and get to their classes after I repaired the courtyard. I went to Katara while William, Yuki, and Kagome stayed with the girl who said her name is Kagura.

WILLIAM

I told Yuki and Kagome to wait by the door while I summoned one of the guards from the palace to come and get Kagura. I looked at Yuki as he said "We are going to continue to protect Haruna until it is time for her to return to Murina." I nodded and turned to the guard then said "You need to take this girl to the palace dungeons for attacking Haruna." He bowed and said "yes my lord" then left with her.

HARUNA

I apologized to Katara "I am sorry, but I am going to have to take a break because I keep bringing trouble to you, the students, and staff." She said "it's ok" while hugging me "We don't blame you. It's all the people who are after you who are at fault." I said "You're right, thank you. I'll see you later" then walked to the door of the hall right as William, Yuki, and Kagome returned. William asked "Where are you going?" I said "home, I am taking a break from teaching." He looked at Yuki and Kagome then said "ok, see you later. Be careful." I said "I will" and went home.

I cleaned up the mansion then went to bed. When I woke up, I started to rake the yard and noticed a makeshift hut in the woods not far from my yard. I walked up to it and saw William, Yuki, and Kagome were fast asleep in it. After I finished, I went back to the hut to check on them. I saw they are awake now and asked "Why are you in a hut in the woods behind my house?"

WILLIAM

We jumped at the sound of her voice and said "sorry, we have actually been watching over you for years." She said "It is ok, I figured you were watching over me when I found you in this hut while you were sleeping earlier. However, you should have told me. You can stay in my mansion instead of sleeping in this hut and watch over me that way." I said "very well" and started to walk to her mansion with her.

HARUNA

I started to walk to the mansion with them when I suddenly sensed Yamato's presence. I stopped and yelled "DON'T MOVE!" and shot fire in the area in front of me. Yamato *appeared and tried to counterattack. I dodged and said "you will have to try harder than that to blindside me" while smiling ecstatically. He said "I see you have grown stronger since I last saw you."*

I said "it is because you have been sending people after me instead of coming yourself for the past fourteen years." He said "yes, that is my fault because I had to recuperate and train after your last attack, but I see it wasn't enough." He looked at me for a while and said "you are also filled with hatred toward me for killing Haru and Elie all those years ago."

I said "exactly, now prepare to die." He said "you will not kill me because I will kill your friends behind you before you can even reach me." He then disappeared and reappeared between us. I yelled "DON'T TOUCH THEM!" and made vines wrap around him and started to suffocate him.

WILLIAM

I rushed to her and said "no, you don't want to do this. If you, do you will be no better than he is and will never forgive yourself." She said "I'll kill him now. He should never have threatened you guys, especially you" with rage and tears in her eyes. I said "I am sorry but I can't let you do this" and hit the back of her neck and caught her as she passed out.

CHAPTER 16

We took her inside her mansion and put her in her bed. I told Kagome and Yuki to guard the mansion while I stayed with her. I sat a chair beside her bed and started to watch her sleep.

HARUNA

I woke up to William looking at me. I asked "Where am I?" He said "you are in your bed in your room." I said "what became of Yamato after you knocked me out?" He looked at me with an apologetic look and said "I had to knock you out because you started to lose control of yourself and would have regretted killing Yamato. He got away but was severely injured." I said "thank you, you know me very well."

WILLIAM

I looked at her and said "Haruna, I need to tell you something." She said "what is it?" I said "the day Haru and Elie were killed I was actually sent there to help protect you by order of my mother and father. I had guards follow me from a distance that day so you would not know I am the prince of

Romora." There is one thing they did not count on though." she asked "what is it?" I said "they did not count on me falling in love with you. Haruna, I have been in love with you since the day we bumped into each other. Although I didn't know you were the girl I had to protect until I met Haru and Elie, who told me you were in danger."

HARUNA

I was shocked to hear him say he loved me because I have always loved him since we first met too and said "that is ironic because I have also loved you since that day as well." He smiled at me then looked at the floor and looked up saying "there is another thing I need to tell you." I said "what else?" he said "you already know I am the prince of Romora but don't know everything about Yuki and Kagome. They are my most trusted bodyguards and best friends. I have had them watch over you while I was not in the villages, Burruna and Alorrur, my mother and father allowed me to let them watch over you." I said "I figured you were a prince when I saw you in the back of the dojo then announced at the talent show at the end of my fourth grade year."

WILLIAM

I looked at her with amusement because I had no idea, she would figure it out unless I told her. she looked at me and said "so, we both love each other" laughed then continued "do you think we should get together since we both love each other?"

I said "yes, I would love to date you and I will never let you go" with a huge smile. I looked at her as she smiled at me and kissed her tenderly.

HARUNA

We worked around the mansion to keep it maintained and planted some flowers in the courtyard. We went to mother and fathers' graves when we were done then went to the market for food and supplies when we needed them. I said "we should go check on Kyo and see how he and his men are doing." they agreed and when we saw everything was fine, started to head home.

CHAPTER 17

I looked at William as we returned to my mansion and said "it has been a month since I took a break from teaching, and I am surprised no one has tried to attack me so; I will go back and check on everyone. I am going to go back tomorrow since it is late." He said "ok, we will go with you." I said "very well but we need to get a good night of sleep." They said "ok" and went to sleep after we ate and bathed.

KATARA

School started with the students behaving badly again. Ever since a month ago when Haruna took a break, they have behaved as if they didn't have a care in the world and now one of the students have brought a match to school and took it to the cafeteria and somehow caused the school to burst into flames. I had everyone get the injured and get out of the building while Kyo and his men came. I told everyone "Stay calm and get to the front of the school."

HARUNA

We were halfway to the school when I noticed smoke in the distance and said "oh no.... by the direction and distance of the smoke, I would say the school is on fire and by the amount of smoke.... shoot." I turned to William, Yuki, and Kagome as I continued "We need to get to the school now. It is on fire again and it is worse than the last one." They said "understood" and started to run.

We reached the school and noticed everyone was in the road in front of the school but there is no sign of Katara. Rema saw us coming and yelled "Haruna! Someone grabbed Katara and dragged her next to the school!" She started crying as she continued "please help her!" I said "Yuki, Kagome help the students. I am going after whoever grabbed Katara. William, help me if I start to have trouble with whoever it is." He said "ok" and went to the side of the school while Yuki and Kagome went to the students to start healing the injured.

I got to the side of the school where Katara was taken and wasn't surprised to see Jiro holding her while she tried to run to me. I said "let her go and you won't get hurt." He said "No because now that I know she is precious to you, I am going to take her with me." I yelled "No you won't!" and ran up to him and grabbed Katara by her arm then ran toward the front of the school while Jiro ran after us. I yelled "William! protect Katara while I deal with Jiro!" He said "will do" and ran in front of Katara after she ran behind him.

I then turned around and waited for him to reach me. Once he did, I ran at him and started to hit his pressure points with enough strength to knock him out and immobilize him without killing him. When he still didn't give up after he could not move his arms and one of his legs, I hit him in the back of his neck. He hit the ground hard and was out cold. William then wrapped vines around him and sat him beside Katara who had sat down from exhaustion.

CHAPTER 18

They used buckets of water from a nearby river to fight the fire as I said "William and I will help you put out the blaze again. Yuki and Kagome are already helping the paramedics with the injured students. He said "ok, we are definitely going to need your help this time." We had the fire under control a while later and put it out an hour later. William looked at me after we put it out and asked "do you want to live with me at my palace for a while? my mother and father have been wanting to meet you and we also need to take Jiro to the palace dungeon because he will be too much trouble for the guards to handle."

I said "yes I will go with you but I am going to have to tell Katara and my neighbors I am going." He said "I understand" and followed me to Katara. I said "Katara, if you have any more trouble at the school you will have to try to deal with it yourself." She asked "Why? You are the reason the students listen in the first place. Why are you saying this now?" I said "because I am moving to Romora with William, Yuki, and Kagome for a while, so I won't be able to protect the school. I will come by for visits and look after and visit mother and father's graves so we will be seeing each other again." She said "ok, have a great time in Romora."

I nodded and started to walk to my neighbor's house. William had Yuki carry Jiro while we walked to my house to pack before going to my neighbors. We finished packing little things that we needed for the long walk to Romora and went to the neighbors. I said "I am going to live with William, Yuki, and Kagome in Romora for a while. Can you make sure no one buys my mansion because I will come back for visits and will need to stay in it. I will continue to make payments for it and I am also going to keep my main belongings in it so it will be locked while I am away. We might move back here later so please do not let anyone try to sell it."

They said "we do not want anyone to sell it either so we will not let anyone try to. We will also make sure the no one tries to steal anything from it. So go have a great time in Romora and be careful getting there." I said "don't worry we will" and started the long walk. I heard Yuki and Kagome ask "Why don't we have horses? It would be faster with them, and we would only have to take a few breaks." he said "because we didn't bring ours here and Haruna does not have a horse" and continued our journey.

CHAPTER 19

I ran through the patch of woods near the path to Romora while chasing Jiro who woke up about half days walk from Alorrur and ran away from us thinking he will escape but little does he know I am chasing him toward William so we can recapture him and continue our walk to Romora. William ran in front of him to block his way while Yuki and Kagome ran beside him after I knocked him out.

I said "I don't know why he thought he would get away from us like he did with your guards last time." William said "he thought he caught us off guard when he jumped off Yuki but I expected him to do that when he woke up so I stayed near Yuki until he woke up." I said "at least we recaptured him. now let's get back to walking so we can get to Romora." They said "ok" and started to walk we were halfway to the area where we were going to make our camp when I noticed out of my peripheral vision, a hawk landing on William's arm than a few minutes later, flew away in front of us.

We walked the rest of the day before making camp and left Kagome to watch Jiro while Yuki and William slept. I was walking around the camp before I finally managed to *fall asleep. I woke up a few hours later to William, Yuki, and Kagome missing. I went into the woods to search for them, when I heard William yell "WATCH OUT HARUNA!!!" I heard movement behind me and dodged a bolt of electricity aimed at me. It was Jiro and he started to come at me again. Right as I was about to deflect his attack, a knight on his horse ran in front of me and started to attack Jiro and sent sparks flying on the first contact with Jiro's sword. Five more came as William, Yuki, and Kagome walked toward me. The captain of the knights said "lord William, we have brought four horses as you requested. I have also brought five knights along with myself to accompany you, Yuki, Kagome, and lady Haruna to the palace. Haruhi and Sasuke will handle Jiro while we are on our travels."*

William said "nice job, I thought we were in trouble that time. You guys have perfect timing." He said "Yes well, we left directly after we received your message from your hawk." I said "So that is what I saw back there. your hawk came to you with a message from your knights and replied to them." William said "Yes.... I didn't expect Jiro to target you when we were halfway to Romora through." He looked at the leader and said "Renji, if Sasuke had not stopped Haruna from deflecting Jiro's attack when he did, he would have had her. Renji said "We know, it was faint, but we saw electricity flowing on his sword." I said "I did not notice the electricity until Sasuke's sword connected with Jiro's.

He said "Jiro had it where you couldn't see it." William said "Ok, since Sasuke and Haruhi just recaptured Jiro, we can finally continue our walk to Romora." We got on the horses Renji provided for us and continued toward Romora on horseback.

I looked around as we arrived in Romora and was surprised to see all the villagers standing along the side of the road. Renji rode up beside me and said "The villagers look up to prince William and have been waiting patiently for his return." I said "Ok, I understand that, but it doesn't explain why everyone is staring at me." he said "they have known about you ever since they learned about prince William staying in Alorrur to watch over you." I said "so they already accept me...." He said "Yes" then looked at the palace as he continued "we will take the horses to the stables and return to our duties. You will need to follow his highness when we get to the palace." I shook my head in understanding and got off my horse to start following William.

William said "I will take you to mother and father before I show you around the castle." I said "ok.... but" while deep in thought. He stopped and asked "what?" while looking at me. I looked around and asked "where are Yuki and Kagome?" He said "they will only be with us when we are out traveling. they are training with the other knights with Jiro right now and will come when I send for them. I said "ok" and walked with him to meet his mother and father.

CHAPTER 20

WILLIAM

I walked up to mother and father with Haruna directly beside me and said "This is Haruna Mori and she has agreed to come live with us." Mother said "Excellent, we have been looking forward to get the chance to finally meet you Haruna." She said "It is a pleasure to make your acquaintance." Mother said "William, take Haruna to her room and come back down directly after. We need to take in private." I said "Yes mother" and started to walk to Haruna's room.

HARUNA

I made sure to notice where everything is as we made our way to my room. He said "We made sure your room is safe and made it in one of the palace towers. Hopefully you will like it." I said "It doesn't matter where it is or what it looks like as long as it has a bed I can sleep on and room for me to change clothes." He said "Do not worry, you will definitely like it seeing how it is the most beautiful room in the palace." I smiled as I walked with him. Before we went up the staircase which led to my room, we stopped in front of a room near the staircase. I was surprised to hear him say "This is my room. I wanted your room close to mine so I would be there if anything happened."

I said "That is very thoughtful of you. I will feel a lot safer knowing you are nearby." He smiled and took me up the staircase to my room. He was right I love my room. It may be at the top of a tower, but the setup is amazing. The bed is along one of the walls beside the closet door. There is even a bathroom directly across from the bed. there is a desk in front of the window. There is even a fireplace across from that with a couple of chairs and a stand in between them. I noticed something was off with the wall beside the fireplace and walked over to inspect it. When I realized it was supposed to be the way it is I turned to William and said "I love it. I didn't expect a tower to have much room for everything that is in here or have enough room between the walls to have a secret escape passage."

He looked at me and said "We remodeled it so you would have everything you would need in here. How did you know about the escape passage?" I said "When I went to inspect the wall." He said "Oh…. so that is what you were doing. Well, I must get back to mother and father now. Supper will be in an hour." I nodded as he walked out the room. I started to unpack my belongings and began to wait till it is time for supper.

WILLIAM

I walked down to the throne room wondering what it is mother, and father needed to talk to me in private about. Once

I got to them, mother said "So..... you love Haruna." I said "Yes, how did you know?" She said "I saw the look you gave her. Does she love you back?" I said "Yes, we started dating just before we left Alorrur." She said "Oh... well, we will allow the relationship because she is a princess even if it is of another world." I said "Thank you mother and father. I promise I will do whatever it takes to protect her for the rest of my life." They both said in sync with each other "We know you will." I asked "Is that all you wanted to know?" She said "Yes, you may go "and dismissed me.

I walked to the library within the palace to do some reading before supper and spend more time with Haruna. I started to walk toward her room to check on her when Renji walked up to me and said "It is time for supper." I said "Very well, let me get Haruna and we will be right down." He said "Sorry my lord but her highness wants you and lady Haruna to come to supper separately. She has sent me to get her." I said "Very well" with a sigh and walked to the dining hall.

HARUNA

I started to stand when there was a knock in the door. I opened it to Renji standing in the entrance and said "Her majesty sent me to escort you to the dining room." I said "Thank you" and followed him. Once we were seated the cooks brought in the food. We finished supper and started to leave the dining room when queen Harushia said "Haruna, you can walk around the castle to get used to it. William needs to interrogate Jiro."

I said "thank you, your majesty." She said "You may call me Harushia." I said "yes ma'am and thank you again" then went to the garden to spend some time alone and view the scenery.

I was about to go deeper into the garden when Renji walked up to me and said "You shouldn't be out here by yourself this late. You don't mind if I walk around here with you, do you?" I said "No, I don't mind having company if that's what you're asking. I was just about to go deeper into the garden." He said "It is a very large and beautiful garden." I said "Yes, it is" and continued to walk through it with him.

WILLIAM

I walked down to Jiro with Yuki and Kagome to start interrogating him. We walked to the interrogation cell he is in and started asking questions. Yuki whispered in my ear "Renji is watching over Haruna while we interrogate Jiro." I said "understood. now Jiro... why do you keep trying to capture Haruna?" He asked "Why would I tell you anything?" I said "because I know who she is, and it is my duty to protect her. now tell me why you are after her or I will have Yuki torture you until we get an answer." He said "Even if I wanted to tell you, Yamato would have me killed." I said "If you tell us, we will protect you although you will remain in a cell." He said "Very well, it is better than what is waiting for me "with a relieved expression and continued "You already know she is a princess of Murina but you don't know a very important fact about her."

I asked "what important fact do you mean?" He asked "How did your parents know she was coming to earth in the first place?" I started to wonder how they knew when they never mentioned another world until Haruna was being chased here but how did they know that? Jiro said "The sudden pause tells me you never thought about it. You can ask them yourself because you wouldn't believe me if I tell but I will give you a hint...... You aren't of earth either." I gasped in surprise "what?! I'm not from earth.... You said some of what you agreed so we will protect you however if I find out you lied about me being from another world, I will kill you myself." He said "very well" and was escorted to a cell while Yuki, Kagome, and I went to mother and father to see if what he said is true."

I said "Mother, Father. Jiro was saying he was after Haruna because she is the princess of Murina. There is a very important part he didn't tell me because he said you know what it is." Mother quickly shrugged and said "we don't know" but the look she gave me said otherwise so I said "I know you are lying because he also said I am not from earth either and how did you know she was coming to this world in the first place?" They sighed as they said "we didn't want to tell you because we didn't want to upset you...... you, Yuki, Kagome, your father Yorgan, and I are from Murina as well" she gave me time to let it set in then continued "We were under attack at our palace on Murina. We were overwhelmed and retreated to Haruna's castle. We were protected by queen Serina and king Raden but eventually had to escape to earth. You, Yuki, Kagome, Yorgan, and I are the only ones who survived the attack. We have kept in contact with King Raden and Queen Serina ever since. We learned from them of Haruna being chased here because she is the balance of Murina. She can heal it when it is dying but she can also kill it. Yamato wants to destroy Murina and needs Haruna to do so."

I said "So, we owe Queen Serina and King Raden our lives and what do you mean she is the 'balance of Murina'?" She said "all we know is she is the reason Murina is still alive and enemies are after her." I said "Ok, why did we have to leave Murina if it is our home planet?" They said "We had no choice and don't mention any of this to Haruna. She will learn when the time is right." I said "ok" and started to walk to my room.

HARUNA

We finished walking through the garden when I heard something in the bushes. It has gotten pretty late, and I can't see what made the noise. I looked back and forth at Renji, and the bush then quickly drew my sword when something lunged at Renji. I was a little surprised to hear the sound of metal on metal as I blocked a sword a couple inches from his head. I looked at Renji who is surprised too and said in a stern tone "Renji! Call the guards and help me. we are under attack." He nodded and right as more intruders attacked, he and a couple guards intercepted. The invasion alarm sounded shortly after.

WILLIAM

I was walking past the garden when the alarm sounded, and I heard the sound of fighting. I looked in the direction the sound was coming from and realized its coming from the garden. I was about to run into it remembering that's where Haruna and Renji are but was stopped by Yuki as he said "Don't worry about Haruna. she has Renji and most of the knights with her. The village is also under attack, we need to get there and protect the civilians." I said "ok" and ran toward the village looking behind me along the way.

HARUNA

I hit my scabbard across one of the intruder's head and knocked him out. I turned around and noticed twenty other intruders attacking the knights. I thought `they are not going to be able to handle them all without my help` to myself then focused and raised my right hand, making water wrap around the intruders' forming spheres around them, making sure to leave an air bubble around their head so they won't drown while making sure the knights didn't get wet. I then pointed my other hand toward the water spheres after making them move closer together, as the air around my hand began to heat up, I flicked my fingers and sent a bolt of electricity into the spheres electrocuting them. As they screamed out from pain Renji ran to me and asked "are you hurt?" I said "Just a few scrapes but the fighting isn't over....... The village is also under attack. The knights in the garden need to put the intruders in the dungeon and protect the palace while Renji and I help the others defend the village" after turning to them. They said "yes my lady" and sprang into action while we made our way to the village.

I saw William leading the civilians to safety while Yuki and the others along with Kagome are fighting the attackers. I started to run to help them when I saw William and the civilians, he is leading are now surrounded. I told Renji to help the others while I help William. He went to help Kagome who was having trouble with two of the attackers. I ran to William with my sword in hand and blocked an enemy's attack before he could land a hit on William. He looked at me and knew exactly what to do. We ran in sync attacking the enemy and bypassing the civilians before they could get hurt. When we defeated the last attacker, we learned Yamato had sent them to get both Jiro and I. I was about to tell William I am going to sleep since the knights had everything under control but felt a jolt of electricity go through my body then everything went black.

WILLIAM

I heard a thud behind me and turned to see Haruna unconscious on the ground while someone with a hooded cape on covering his whole body is standing over her. I yelled "RENJI, YUKI, KAGOME!!!!! Haruna is in trouble!" Yuki ran to and grabbed her to get her out of the way while we charged at him but did not get close enough to him before he suddenly disappeared. I turned to Yuki who still has ahold of her and asked "Is she ok?" He said "Yes, she is just unconscious" after checking her head for any blood from whatever she was hit with. I said "that's good" with a sigh and continued "we should take her to her room and station a guard in front of her stairway until she comes to." They said "ok" and walked with me to her room.

Renji said "I'll stand guard if that's alright with you, lord William." I said "yes, it is fine with me besides Yuki and Kagome, you are among my most trusted knights along with Haruhi and Sasuke." I started to think of the other two knights who came to rescue and escort us and added "I also trust Namine and Kaoru." He said "that is true, my lord" and began to stand watch as we placed Haruna in her futon. We watched over her all night while the other knights repaired the damage done to the village during the attack.

CHAPTER 21

HARUNA

    I woke to Yuki sitting in one of the chairs in front of the fireplace. I asked after sitting up "what happened? How did I get to my room?" He looked at me with relief in his eyes and said "I am glad you are finally awake. You have been unconscious for a week. Everyone is fine. The attackers are still in the dungeon. They ended up being threatened by Yamato and had no choice but to attack us. We will let them go when they finish their sentence which is a month in the dungeon. I will send word for William to come and see you. He hasn't been able to focus lately because he has not stopped worrying about you since the attack." I said "wait...... I have been asleep for a week......." He said "yes, we don't know what hit you to knock you out so long but there was a man in a hooded cape standing over you." I said "I know what hit me....... it was lightning...... at least felt like it. Did you get whoever was standing over me?" He said "no, He disappeared before we could get him."

    I said "Ok, go get William. I need to change out of my night clothes." I started to think and said "wait... how did I get into my night clothes in the first place?" He said "We had one of the female attendants dress you. Your other clothes had to be replaced because you cut your head and arms when you fell. The blood got absorbed into them and you are lucky you heal fast." I said "Ok, thank you" and started to change after he left.

William burst into the room a short while later and immediately hugged and kissed me, then said "I'm relieved you are alright. When you didn't wake up, I got worried. Yuki said you think it was lightning that hit you. How do you know?" I said "because I felt a jolt just before I passed out." He said "We will find whoever did that to you and make them pay" with rage in his tone. I said "don't worry about it. Everything should be fine now." He said "it is, do you want to go for a horse ride? You need to get out after sleeping so long." I said "yes, let's go right now" with a smile. He said "no, we need to eat first" as my stomach growled. I said "ok" and followed him to the dining room while feeling a little embarrassed.

We ate a very delicious meal of porridge and rice then went to the stables to get our horses ready. I looked at William and asked "are Yuki and Kagome coming along?" He said "yes, they are waiting for us at the forest entrance." I said "ok let's go then." He said "very well, let's meet up with them." We got on our horses and got to the forest. They looked at us and said "You two sure took your time. There was a little girl with medium length hair and a light green dress on walking around the edge of the forest. Once you two came into view she vanished." I looked at William then back at them and asked "what color hair did she have?" Yuki said "brown why?" I said "can't quite put my finger on it but we need to tell her it isn't safe if we see her again." They said "you're right, well let's get through the woods."

We got halfway through when we heard a little girl scream "LEAVE ME ALONE!!!!" We looked in her direction to see if she needed help and was surprised to see two grown men and a bear unconscious on the ground. We asked "did you do this?" right before she said "yes I did this and will not tell you why." I said "you shouldn't be alone in the woods even if you can defend yourself." She said "I know" then vanished as if she was never there to begin with.

We looked at each other in confusion as I said "I knew she had powers when I saw the unconscious men and bear but never expected she would be able to manipulate nature to make herself disappear." William said "same here but we should probably get back to the castle before that bear wakes up. We should give the horses a break and walk them back." I said "agreed, they look exhausted, and I need to walk a little."

As we were walking, William said "I have been thinking it is about time we returned to Alorrur." I said "ok, how long?" He said "permanently. We can ask mother and father if we can bring some knights to guard your mansion." I said "ok, we need to visit mother and fathers' graves when we get back too." They nodded and continued to the palace then put the horses back in their stalls at the stables.

We talked to Yurgan and Harushia who said "we will allow you to go back if you let us pick which knights go with you and you can take some horses too." I said "very well, thank

Alyssia Clemmer

you for letting us go back to Alorrur." They said "We knew you
would go back sooner or later.... now sleep tonight and leave
tomorrow. We will have the knights wait for you at the front
gate in the morning."

I said "as you wish, good night and we will have a safe
journey back to Alorrur." They said "good night" as we left
the throne room. William said "I hope they don't pick too
much knights to accompany us." I said "yea, I know Yuki and
Kagome are coming with us since they are our bodyguards but
who else are they going to pick?" He said "I don't know but we
will find out in the morning and like whoever they pick." I said
"yes well, we better get some sleep. so, I am going to head to
bed. good night." He said "good night" and went to his room. I
packed for the trip home then went to sleep.

CHAPTER 22

WILLIAM

I woke to Yuki looking at me and asked "what is wrong?" He said "Kagome is getting Lady Haruna. I have been sent to get you. Queen Harushia and King Yurgan have requested your and lady Haruna's presence in the throne room before we leave." I said "ok, let's get down there then." We got down there and were surprised to see mother and father being held captive with swords to their throats. I started to think of something to do but was grabbed from behind and now have a sword against my throat. I looked at Yuki and Kagome and saw they are also subdued. I realized Haruna is still free though and on guard.

HARUNA

I looked around at everyone and said "everything will be alright. I won't let them do anything to you." Someone said from behind me "I know you will do anything for those you hold dear so, you had better come with us." I turned around and saw the leader of a local band of mercenaries. I said "Who do you think you are threatening my family." He said "I am the leader of the Masunas Mercenary band and we want you in our group because we have seen how skilled you are with a sword." I said "That doesn't mean you can come into the castle and put the royal family and my friends to the blade in order to get me to join your mercenary band. All you would have had to do was ask me directly." He said "We were going to but found out you were leaving to live in Alorrur."

I said "I will join your mercenary band if you let everyone go but if you don't I will kill you where you stand." He gulped and said "very well, sorry it ended up this way." I said "its ok and tell me your name so I will know who to ask for when I go to your headquarters." He said "I am Kyjo, now let everyone go" after he turned to his men. One of them accidentally knicked Kagome's neck and that was all it took to make me lose control even though it was an accident. I ran to the man who knicked her and sent him flying across the room.

WILLIAM

I saw her eyes turn red then kick the young man who just accidentally knicked Kagome. I yelled "YUKI, CATCH HIM!!!" Yuki was already running at him and managed to catch him before he could hit the wall. I then started to run to Haruna. Kyjo asked "why is she doing this?" in confusion and surprise. I said while still running "She lost control of her anger when she saw your companion accidentally Knick Kagome. If I don't calm her down now, she will kill him. He said "oh no....... Now I know not to get her mad." I said "your first mistake was putting us to the blade. now if you don't mind, I am going to calm her down before she kills your friend."

I got to Haruna and stood between her and the boy she is after. I then said "You don't want to do this. You need to calm down before you do something you'll regret." She said "why should I when they threatened you and everyone else?" I said "he didn't mean to hurt Kagome and they felt this was their only chance to ask you and became desperate. They weren't going to hurt anyone." She looked at me for a few moments which felt longer and once I saw her eyes turn back to their normal sky blue, knew she had finally calmed down and breathed a sigh of relief.

HARUNA

I looked at Kyjo and said "if you ever threaten anyone I hold dear to me again it won't be your men who will be in danger, it will be you." He looked at me in terror and said "understood, we will never threaten anyone close to you again." I looked at Queen Harushia and asked "are you alright? I'm sorry this happened." she said "no worries, no one was killed, and they were desperate so we will overlook this. now back to the matter at hand, we have chosen Renji, Haruhi, Sasuke, Namine, and Kaoru to go protect your mansion.... of course, Yuki and Kagome are going with you too since you never go anywhere without them. Have a safe journey to Alorrur and be sure to visit us occasionally."

I said "don't worry we will. You be sure to stay safe too" then looked at Kyjo and continued "I will be sure to visit your *headquarters to officially join the Masunas." He said "very well" and walked away with his men. I looked at Harushia and said "we will be on our way as well. Please be safe when we are gone." She said "don't worry, we will. Now get going...... you have a long journey ahead of you. Everyone is waiting at the gate." I said "ok" and started to walk to the front gate with William, Yuki, and Kagome right behind me.*

CHAPTER 23

We got to the gate and was surprised to see nine of the palaces best stallions were being held by Renji and the others. Renji walked up to us and while holding two stallions "Queen Harushia insisted on us taking some of the best stallions with us. They are gifts we can't refuse."

I said "understood" while grabbing the reins of the stallion he is handing me. We mounted and started our journey back to Alorrur. "I am eager to finally get back there and visit mother and father's graves" said I as we galloped. William said "It shouldn't take as long as it took us to walk since we have stallions." I said "Indeed, it should take around one and a half days to get there since we are still going to need to make camp for the stallions to rest." He said "They will definitely need a break and we cannot continuously ride them without giving them time to rest. It would kill them if we did" and continued on.

We got to an area where we made camp and gave the stallions a rest. I looked at William and said "I am going to go for a short walk in the nearby woods. I will be back in a short while." He looked at Yuki then back at me and said "do you want someone to accompany you?" I said "No, I will go alone this time" then walked to the forest following the hunch I had.

WILLIAM

I looked at Yuki and was about to tell him to follow her, but he shook his head and said "already on it" then began to sneak into the forest. I looked at Kagome and said "We will wait for them to return before we go to sleep." she said "understood and that is what I was thinking already" and returned to our campfire.

HARUNA

I saw Yuki climb a tree and start to follow me through them. I knew he would be there, so I began to work my way to the middle of the forest." I said "I had a feeling you would follow me" and put my hand behind my back signaling Yuki to stay knowing he would think I was talking to him. He stayed put and began to watch me and the surrounding area.

Kyjo walked out from behind a tree a short distance in front of me and said "you have sharp eyes" with a grin. I said "of course I do. There is not much I miss. I knew you and your men would follow me to try to figure out where I live in Alorrur." He grimaced and said "you don't understand. We didn't follow you to keep tabs or figure out where you live. We followed you to take you away from prince William and the others to force you to join the Masunas early and become my wife....... You will be mine."

I said "I am sorry but I love William too much to let him go now and no one will ever tear us apart." He said "You will not be with him much longer. Pretty soon you will be my wife. With your skills and my tactics, we will be unstoppable." I said "that will never happen, and you are not the only one who knows tactics. I love him too much and will never give him up. No matter how much you want to take me away, you can't." I started to turn away and return to camp but was grabbed by him and started to get dragged toward his men.

I looked at Yuki and mouthed 'now' and watched as he dove out of his tree and hit Kyjo's arms, making him stagger and release me from his grasp. I turned to him and said "Did you really think I came alone when in truth I am never alone. There is another thing you don't know about me............" He said "I know everything about you my dear" before I could finish. I felt my rage reach a boiling point and knew my eyes were about to turn red and make me lose control again then said "No you don't. There is very little you know about me" and started to charge at him sword in hand. Kyjo had a mixture of fear and shock in his eyes when Yuki had jumped in front of me and grabbed my arm then said "calm down, you don't want to do this and he isn't worth it anyway."

I looked at him and calmed down. I felt the rage leave my body and said "you are right as always just like William and Kagome although you are always right. I don't want to do this." I looked at Kyjo and said "as I was saying .... you know very little about me or anyone else I travel with" and lifted my hand making the ground shift below their feet. A circular ditch was created around them and branches of the nearby trees above them came down and wrapped around them trapping them and not allowing them to move from the space they are in. I looked him dead in the eyes and said "William, Yuki, Kagome, and I are rare beings in this world known as sacred beings. We have the ability to manipulate and control the elements around us although Yuki and Kagome can't control all of them like William and I can. We are the only ones who can. Now you and your men will be in that cage until the knights from the palace come get you."

I whistled for my fox friend who for some reason always followed me since as long as I can remember and when she walked up to me, I leaned down to her and asked "Lancer, I need your help. I need you to take this note to the palace in Romora." She looked at me with eagerness in her eyes and shook her head. I said "I need you to carry this note so they will know what to do" as she carefully took the note from my hand I continued "I have written they need to follow you along with a few other things so don't leave until they are prepared to follow you." She shook her head once more and ran toward Romora.

I turned to Yuki who watched as I sent Lancer away and said "don't look at me like that. I knew you would follow me since you are my bodyguard, even when we were staying at the palace, you would constantly check up on me and when I was knocked out you stayed by my side, besides I needed to confront them. If I didn't, they would have followed us to my mansion." He said "I understand but you were being reckless none the less." I said "I know and I will explain everything to William and the others when we get back to camp." He said "you better because if you don't, I will" and followed me back to camp.

William looked our way as we walked toward him and asked "did something happen? You took a while in the forest." I said "yes and we can't leave camp yet. We encountered the Masunas in the forest. They tried to force me to join them early and make me Kyjos wife but we stopped them and trapped them with the trees and ground around them. I have sent word to queen Harushia to send some knights to take them to the dungeon so we need to wait for them, and I am the only one who can release them from my cage." He said "very well, we will leave after they take them away." I said "they were the reason I went for that walk. I had a feeling they would follow us and knew if I went into the forest alone, Yuki would follow so we ambushed them although I called out to them, Yuki stayed put until I gave him the signal." He said "I knew there was a reason behind your stroll" and smiled at me.

WILLIAM

We noticed ten knights approaching on their stallions following Lancer. When they got closer, I noticed mother is among them. I walked over to her and said "mother, you came too. You know it isn't safe for you to be out of the palace." She said "I know but I saw the message we received from Haruna's silver fox messenger who brought us here.... now where are those troublesome Masunas?"

HARUSHIA

Haruna walked up to us and said "my messengers name is Lancer, and she just became my messenger when she brought you, my letter. For some reason she always follows me so I thought of making her my messenger and I will take you to them as I said in the note. I made a cage around them, and I am the only one who can undo it."

WILLIAM

Mother said "Lancer is a good name for her and lets go get them." I followed them to a meadow with a cage along the edge. Haruna undid the cage while the knights who accompanied mother put shackles around their wrists then shackled them to each other. Mother said "you should have never tried to pull William and Haruna apart. Those two are inseparable." she then looked at us and said "you can continue on your journey now" then proceeded back to the palace with them.

CHAPTER 24

HARUNA

We packed up our camp and continued our journey to Alorrur after we watched queen Harushia and her ten knights fade into the distance. When we finally got back to my mansion, I wasn't surprised to see my neighbors walk up to me and say "welcome back, we kept your lawn cut and made sure no one went near your mansion. we did just as you asked three months ago. how long will you be here?" I said "it is good to be back. We are moving back here so you will not have to watch over the mansion anymore."

They said "Ok, if you are out on business we will look after it." I said "You don't have to do that. There will always be knights guarding it from now on." They said "We will still watch over it even with the guards now. We helped build it so we will continue to take care of it while you are gone. It is the least we can do." I said "If you insist then go ahead as long as you want to." They said "We want to and thank you" before returning to their home. Renji walked up to me after we closed the gate to ensure the stallions didn't run away and said "you built this mansion? Now that is impressive.

I said "Yes, this used to be a rundown old house but mother and father bought it and started to rebuild and remodel it and after they were murdered by Yamato I continued their work with the help of my neighbors, the Yarashia's, and this is what it became. Now I need to get materials to start building a stable for the stallions. I can visit mother and fathers' graves after I finish building it." he said "very well" and stayed behind to stand guard while I went to the market with William, Yuki, and Kagome.

We got to the market and split up into two groups to get the supplies and materials we need for the stables. Yuki came with me to get the wood and stone while William and Kagome went to get hay and feed for the stallions and nails and puddy for the structure itself. We met up a short time later and walked back to the mansion to start on the stables. With the Yarashia's, Renji, William, and everyone else there to help, it didn't take long to finish.

We put the stallions in their stalls and went inside to eat and get ready for bed. While we were eating Kagome said "I am surprised it didn't take us longer to build the stables." I said "yes, when it was just the Yarashia's and I, it took us years to finish the mansion but it only to us two days with the help of everyone here." William said "Yes, I am sorry I didn't help you before, but we were watching over you without your knowledge back then."

Renji looked at me and asked "When are you going to visit your parents graves?" I said "Tomorrow after everyone wakes up and eats breakfast then we are also going to visit Katara and her students to see how everything is going." William said "Ok.... Kagome, Yuki, and I will go with you like always." I nodded and continued eating. Namine asked "What is wrong with the school?" I finished eating and said "before I worked there, the kids always fought each other. Katara greeted me once I arrived because Susan, the middle school principal, had already told her about me and I have been helping her teach at the dojo and break up fights ever since."

She said "Oh....ok, now I understand." I said "Yes and now I am going to bed now that I am done eating. Good night, everyone, see you tomorrow." They said "good night" as I walked out the room. I woke up to Yuki walking into the room. He said "I was wondering when you would wake up. Everyone is already awake. They are waiting for you to come down to eat." I said "I'll be down in a few" and went down after I changed. I was surprised to find a lot of villagers shouting "Happy Birthday" to me. William walked up to me and said "did you really think we wouldn't know when your birthday is? We decided to give you a surprise party. Happy nineteenth birthday babe."

HARUNA

I said "Thank you and I have never worried about you forgetting my birthday because I have not celebrated it since mother and father were murdered. Thank you for the thought of giving me a party though. It really cheered me up." William said "it is good we got you cheered up and your birthday is important no matter what happens on it. We can still visit Haru and Elie after the party. It is only a few hours long." I said "very well, I will spend some time with everyone." He said "good" and spent the next few hours with the guests.

I walked up to William after everyone left. He said "We can go visit Haru and Elie now." I said "let's go" turned to Renji and said "We are going to the graveyard and Katara now. Please watch over the mansion while we are gone." He said "Will do" and got everyone into their stations. We got to the graveyard and stood around mother and fathers graves. I kneeled down and said "I'm back mother and father. Sorry I haven't visited in a while. I moved back to the mansion four days ago. Now that we live here again, I will visit as much as I can. I am going to visit Katara to see how everything is going. I will come to visit again soon. Bye for now, I love you mother and father."

As we were leaving the graveyard, I heard a voice and looked at the others. I noticed they heard it too. We looked behind us and saw mother and fathers' ghosts looking at us. Mother said "We knew you were watching over her when we saw you two in the tree all those years ago. Now please watch over her as you always do you three." William said "Don't worry, I will continue to no matter what." I said "I knew you two were guarding me while I stayed in the graveyard." They said "We knew you sensed us and enjoyed every minute you spent here." I said "same here" while smiling "We are going to see Katara now. See you two later." They said "be careful on your way there." I said "we will" and walked out the graveyard.

CHAPTER 25

We were almost to the school when I saw the flames and smoke. I said "The school is on fire again and it is worse than the others were. We need to put the fire out before it spreads." We started to run toward it when Yuki asked "What about everyone who goes there?" William looked at me and said "They made it out, there is no one inside" after he watched me scan the area. Yuki smiled as Kagome said "thank goodness" and continued running.

I saw Katara in the field, when we got to the school, telling everyone to remain calm until Kyo and his men arrive. Everyone listened to her and continued to watch the school burn. Yuki and Kagome said "We are going to help Katara." I said "alright, William and I are going to start getting the fire under control so keep out of the way of the water while making your way to her" and started to control the water from a nearby pond and got it to the fire. Yuki and Kagome jumped out of the way and continued to run to Katara.

The water missed them by mere inches and hit the fire dead on, ten feet in front of them. When everyone followed the water, they saw William and I were controlling it while Yuki and Kagome are running toward them. Katara smiled and yelled

"Haruna and the others are back! Just in the knick of time too!" Some of the new students said "you weren't making things up. She really does have powers and so do her friends." Katara and one of the students who stayed to help after they graduated walked up to them and said "we would never make up stories about them." They continued to watch us until Kyo, and his men finally arrived. Kyo walked up to me and said "Your back and helping the school again. There were three fires other than this one. The road you found all those years ago really helped us out."

I said "thank you and I figured there would be some fires. They only listened because I was there. Now let's put out this fire." He said "yes lets" and brought buckets to the fire. We managed to put it out after a while. I looked at William and said "let's get the building repaired and find out what started the fire." He said "yeah" and repaired the school.

WILLIAM

I looked at Haruna and smiled but became concerned when the earth started to shake around us and heard her scream "There is a fissure opening!!!! Everyone grab something and hold on tight!!!" Everyone grabbed trees and each other. I grabbed a tree behind Haruna and between Yuki and Kagome, but soon realized Haruna is still in the middle of the opening fissure and not holding anything. I was about to run to her when I noticed what it is she is doing. She is attempting to close the fissure before it opens completely and swallows everyone. I yelled "Hold on tight!!!!" and stopped Yuki from running to her.

Everyone watched as her energy burst out around her. They kept their eyes on her when she let out a loud scream. Shortly after, I felt the shaking grow worse as she forced it closed. I realized when she closed it she wasn't using her full strength. She is only using half of her power. When it closed, she started to walk toward us so I started walking toward her but she turned around suddenly and shot fire in the space behind her. I saw a flash and Yuki was directly beside her.

YUKI

I got beside Haruna and noticed the space was no longer empty. Yamato is now in it. Haruna grabbed her sword and said "I knew the fire and fissure weren't normal. You started the fire and opened the fissure also I had a feeling you would heal faster when William knocked me out that day." I watched as Yamato smiled at her and said "you're right, I did catch your precious school on fire but only did it to lure you here and trap you in that fissure, but I have underestimated you yet again...... I guess training isn't enough to beat you because you will only keep getting stronger." She said "I will always be stronger than you so give up already." He said "you're right again...... I think I'll retreat now.... bye "as he disappeared.

HARUNA

I stared dumbfounded for a few seconds and said "Wait, don't be a chicken and run away. Stay and fight me." I started to think and continue in a whisper to myself "or are you trying to get me away from everyone else." He said "I am not running away. I am simply going into the forest, come if you dare." Yuki got out of his fighting stance and watched as William ran to me and asked "Are you alright? Was he behind everything? Why did he run away?" I said "yes, he was, and he ran away daring me to follow and don't worry I am safe. Yuki had my back." He looked at me with a worried look and asked "you're not going after him are you?" I said "not right now. I have everyone else to worry about."

William walked to Katara with a sad expression. I walked up to Kyo and said "thank you for watching the school while I was gone." He said "your welcome. I will do anything for you since I owe you, my life. If you didn't pull me out of that burning watermill when you did all those years ago, I wouldn't be here today." I said "you should listen to your surroundings, and I will never have to pull you out of a situation like that ever again" while smiling. He said "yes....... I must go. Need to get back to the station." I said "Ok, bye" and walked over to Katara. I talked to her for a while before she left to go home. I told William "I am going into the forest. Walk home with Yuki and Kagome while keeping an eye on my aura." He said "very well" as he watched me leave.

WILLIAM

When Haruna was out of sight I told Yuki to follow her. He said "On it....... I was going to even if you didn't tell me to" then ran in her direction while we went home.

CHAPTER 26

HARUNA

 I entered the woods and started to wonder where he could have gone. I got halfway through the forest when I heard footsteps running toward at me from behind. I turned around to find the little girl we saw in the forest around Romora in front of me. She said "Haruna! The person you are looking for is behind that tree. He attacked me but I got away."

 I looked at the tree ten feet in front of me and saw Yamato walk out from behind it. I said "let me handle this." She said "understood" with a determined expression. He started to walk closer to us and said "So..... you finally decided to come to me." I said "You know I will never forgive you for everything you have done." He said "I know" while lunging at the little girl and I. I blocked him and said "Get to cover, hurry." She ran toward a hollow tree behind us as Yamato went to grab her. I grabbed his arm and flung him into a nearby tree.

 I continued fighting him while protecting the girl. He shot fire at me, but I deflected it and shot it back at him. He abruptly stopped when it hit his arm and looked at the girl then back at me with an evil grin. I yelled "NO" as he turned toward her and shot lightning at her. I thought 'No, I'm not going to make it' and was amazed to see her maneuver the branches to make a lightning rod to absorb the lightning.

She yelled "Leave me out of this! This is a fight between you and Haruna." I fought him for two hours and started to feel tired. Yamato was also getting tired. I lunged at him but was knocked to the ground. I am now severely injured but refuse to give up. I am trying to get up but can barely move and can feel myself starting to slip away. As Yamato walks toward me, I start to think 'am I going to die or is he going to take me away like he was going to back then? If I die, I hope William will handle it easily or will he not stop until he gets revenge?' I said "Sorry........ Willi...am" and could barely keep my eyes open as I began to fall unconscious.

I noticed he was now close to me. I tried to move but can't anymore. I said "cr... ap...." as I started closing my eyes. As I was about to fall unconscious, I saw someone in a black cloak jump in-between Yamato and I and said "you aren't going to hurt her anymore." I said "that...voi.... ce...R...e... n...." He said "it's ok, Haruna. You are safe now" then everything went black.

REN

I looked at my little sister as she said "she is unconscious" after she came out of the hollow tree. I said "I thought I told you not to reveal yourself to her. Luna, you should have listened."

She said "She doesn't remember us Ren." I said "she remembers my name and you were being selfish." She said "I know, but I am staying with her until we go back to Murina." I said "fine, now let me deal with Yamato." She said "yes brother" and watched as I said "now for your punishment Yamato. May you be imprisoned in the abyss forever" and opened a portal which dragged him in and disappeared.

YUKI

I finally managed to catch up to Haruna to find the cloaked man from Romora standing in front of her and the little girl from the forest kneeling beside him while holding Haruna's hand. He turned toward me and said "She is safe. I stopped Yamato from capturing her. Luna is going to watch over her while you go get William and Kagome." I said "So the little girl is Luna but who are you?" He said "I am a friend, that's all you need to know for now." I asked "why did you try to capture her in Romora?" He said "I wanted to take her home so she wouldn't be in danger anymore. Now go get them while Luna protects her." I nodded and went to get them as he disappeared.

HARUNA

I woke to find myself leaned against a boulder surrounded by wildlife. There is also the little girl from earlier curled up against a deer with its fawn beside her. There are a couple wolves, mice, foxes, and owls too. She woke up as if she knew I am awake and said "Everything is fine. I am watching you until Yuki gets back with the others. I'm Luna by the way." I said "Luna is a wonderful name." She said "I know and I have decided to travel with you from now on." I said "OK if that's what you want to do" then started thinking "what happened to...." "Yamato?" she cut in "he won't be bothering you ever again." I said "OK and how do you know his name." "I know his name because I have been watching you and knew he was after you," said she.

I looked into the distance and saw them running toward us. I said "alright" and stood up. Luna said "you were hurt pretty badly so I used my powers to heal you." I said "thank you", looked at William, and continued "we need to get back to the school and see if everyone is ok." He said "OK, but we can't go right now, we need to make camp here for the night and let you rest and regain your strength." I said "very well" and got some sleep after they set up camp.

CHAPTER 27

I woke to William placing rice balls on the stand beside my futon in my tent and started to eat. While I ate, Yuki and Kagome patrolled the perimeter of the camp. When I finished eating, I said "we need to go check on Katara and see if they are ok. After what happened yesterday, I am worried about them." He said "I'm worried too.... let's go." We packed up our camp and grabbed the stallions then started walking with them to the school.

When we got to the school, we started to get worried because no one was there. We searched around everywhere in the school but found no one. I looked at William and said "We need to take the stallions home and come back here to figure out what happened." He nodded and rode to the mansion, put the stallions in their stall, watched me put a barrier around the mansion and property, then told the Yarashias about it. I also told them I am putting up another barrier around the graveyard in Burruna. I then went back to the school to start investigating everyone's disappearance.

I told William it would be better if we split up to find clues to what happened here. I went to the office with Yuki while

William searched for clues around the classrooms with Kagome. I closed the door and said "You can come out now." Yuki looked at me and was surprised to see Luna appear beside me. He said "I was wondering where she went when she wasn't with you." She said "I didn't want William and Kagome to see me just yet so I manipulated the wind to turn me invisible." He said "Ok, now I understand your power is the manipulation of wind." she said "yes.... and nature" and looked at me as I said "we need to figure out what happened here" and started to scan the area for any abnormalities. I found a change in the atmosphere in the office and realized what happened.

I said "I know what happened.... We need to find William and Kagome to explain what happened to everyone and what we need to do." he said nodded and followed me to them. I said "Everyone was transported somewhere. I don't know where though." William asked "How do you know and why is the little girl from the forest in Romora doing here?" I answered "I scanned the school while we were in the office and noticed the remains of a portal and Luna is a sacred being just like us. She will be traveling with us from now on."

KAGOME

I said "Very well, but how are we going to rescue them if they are in another world?" Haruna said "I am going to open a portal to the world they have been taken to and bring them back. Let's open it in Katara's office." I said "That is a good idea." She opened the portal then said "We do not know where we are going so be on guard now let's go." I agreed and walked into the portal after everyone else. When we reached the end of it, we found ourselves in a vast Jungle.

HARUNA

I sensed something coming and said to William "Something is coming" then looked in the direction it is coming from and realized there were two sabertoothed tigers running straight at us. I yelled "Brace Yourselves!!!" Luna walked in front of us with a smile and said "It is ok, they are not going to hurt us. Haruna, you really don't remember this world, do you?" I said "wait.... what do you mean?" she said "you will soon remember everything" and looked at the sabertoothed tigers coming our way.

I watched as they stopped in front of Luna and I. Luna said "Yuna, it's good to see you again. I have missed you so much." she said "I missed you too" and started to rub up against her as she started to get her fur stroked. I was surprised to hear her speak and said "you spoke." The black one with a white patch on his forehead who stopped in front of me said "you don't remember anything do you Haruna?" William said "this world we are in right now......it's Murina isn't it?" He said "yes" and looked at me. I then remembered William and Jiro said I am the princess of Murina and said "wait.... are you saying we are on the world where I am the princess of...." He said "yes, you know this but nothing else?" William said "I told her she was when I couldn't hide it anymore. She has had people after

99

her since she first stepped on earth and forgot everything except her powers."

He said "I know she was supposed to, now it is time for you to remember everything. Haruna please kneel down." As I kneeled down, he put his paw on my forehead and I began to feel his aura flow into me. I stood up and said "Thank you Kiba" looked at William then continued "this is in fact Murina. Now let me explain everything. I was in danger so my real mother and father, Queen Serina and King Raden, had me escape to earth with Elie and Haru posing as my parents while I forgot everything about Murina except my powers until it was safe to return but it back fired on us when Yamato learned of our plan and followed us to Earth. Kiba is my familiar and Yuna is Lunas. you, Kagome, and Yuki have familiars too........... but they are in the palace dungeon."

William said "Ok, now I understand why it is our family's duty to protect you but why are our familiars in the dungeon?" I said "because when a familiar loses their other half, as known as, their companions they start to lose control of themselves until they are reunited but some like Kiba and Yuna never lose themselves and can go years without being beside their other half, although they still don't like to be separated and try to stay by our sides." He said "Oh.... then we need to reunite with them." I said "yes and I left one thing out........" He asked "what?" as he looked at me. I said "Luna is my younger sister." He yelled "WHAT!?" and looked at her. I said "don't look so surprised. She got worried and began to watch over me. I also have a brother but don't know where he is right now. The last time I saw him was back on Earth" after I thought about Katara and everyone else I continued "let's get mother and father to help us find them." He said "good idea" and followed Kiba and I to the palace.

CHAPTER 28

I said as we walked to the palace "there is something about sabertooths you need to know, only sacred beings have sabertoothed tigers as familiars. Their color and way their fur is depends on which elements their masters can control. Since I can control all elements and am the balance of Murina, Kiba is black with a white patch on his forehead and since you can control all the elements as well your familiar, Nora, is like Kiba but is white with a black patch on her forehead. Yuki, your familiar Bita, is red with white markings. Kagome yours known as Ruka, is white with blue markings. My brother Ren's familiar is blue with yellow markings and is known as Fang and of course you can see Yuna is brown with a white tint to it while her markings are green."

He asked "Why do sacred beings get sabertooths? Is there a specific reason?" I said "We get them because they can help us the most although the true reason is unknown but we do know it involves the fact of sacred beings being immortal." He said "If we are immortal, why do we get hurt so badly and get close to dying?" I said "because we can get injured and fall into a deep sleep but never die. That is our burden alone to bare." I remembered something and continued "My last name isn't Mori, it's Yoshamada." He said "oh.... I knew your last name wasn't Mori when I found out Haru and Elie weren't your real parents because their last name is Mori." I said "exactly" looked at Runeshia, the village right below Runeshia palace and said "We are here."

I was surprised to see mother and father waiting at the edge of the village with a platoon of knights. When we got to them, mother said "I remembered Kiba said the only reason he would ever leave the castle is to go to you when you finally returned, so when he took off along with Yuna, I knew you two had returned so we came to meet you. Welcome home both of you." The villagers cheered then father spotted William and said "William, it's good to see you and the others again."

He said "it's good to see you too." We started to walk to Runeshia palace and continued talking. I said "mother, father....... I'm sorry Yamato followed us to Earth and killed Haru and Elie. They are buried on Earth." They said "Oh no.... did he follow you here?" I said "No.... He disappeared after Ren stopped him from catching me." I looked down and started to remember Katara and the others then said "I came here to find my friends who were brought here to take them back to earth." She said "We will find them" with a serious look in her eyes.

We made it to the courtyard and was surprised to hear mother and father say they want me to fight the knights to see how well my powers have grown. They had everyone stand near them. One of the knights ran at me. I caught his sword in mine when he swung at my head and looked at mother. She said "don't hold back Haruna. Go full force." When they tried to double team me, I let go of my sword and sent them flying with the wind. They kept adding knights to the fight but could never get close enough to hit me because I kept blowing them away and when they got close, I would dodge them. Mother said "stop holding back." I said "You want to test my strength but if I go full force they will die" while still dodging them.

They kept coming at me and I became fed up with them, so I sent electricity through their swords when they touched mine making them drop them, then made vines subdue them. I looked at mother and father and said "I only kill when I need to and it hasn't happened yet" while walking past the knights and remembered something I learned on Earth then said "and knights or any combatant aren't tools to be used and disposed of as we see fit. They are people too." I then unbound them and started to walk inside. Mother said "the full force of your abilities are amazing. Now let's show everyone to their rooms since they will stay here while you search for your friends." Just as they were going through the door I said "Mother, Father" with a serious expression. After they said "yes dear" I said "That wasn't my full power.... I was holding back."

They said "What!!? You are more powerful than we ever imagined you would be. "I said "yes, if I would have gone full force, I would have destroyed the village and palace." They stopped in their tracks when I said that and went silent with horrified looks. A moment later they said "oh....... the others need to follow us to their familiars before they lose themselves completely." They nodded and followed them while Luna and I went to my room.

CHAPTER 29

WILLIAM

We went to Nora, Bita, and Ruka and were surprised to see them trying to attack us. Queen Serina said "you need to touch their foreheads to stop them from losing it." I watched as Yuki and Kagome rushed at Bita and Ruka and quickly touched their foreheads then sent their aura into them. They quickly came back to their senses but when I tried the same, I couldn't get close enough to Nora to put my hand on her forehead. Bita and Ruka looked at me and said "we will hold her down to buy some time for you. She always gets more aggressive when she loses her senses, but we need to act fast because she is dangerously close to losing complete control and if that happens you will never get her back."

I said "very well" and waited for them to pounce on her. When they did, I threw myself at her and sent my aura through her forehead. She looked at me as we got off her and said "I almost lost it there but now that I have you back, it will never happen again because I will never leave your side again whether you like it or not." I said "Ok, it's good to finally have you back." She said "same here" and looked at queen Serina as I said "We should get back to Haruna and Luna." She said "very well, I will take you to her after I show you to your rooms." I nodded and followed her to the room she said was Haruna's brothers. After she showed me my room, we went to the barracks and were shown where Yuki and Kagome will sleep. We then went to Haruna's room.

HARUNA

I looked at my door as I heard them open it and looked at mom then said "Thank you for bringing them to me." She said "You are welcome, now I know you need to find your friends so I will leave and let you discuss whatever it is you are going to do, good night." We said "good night" as she closed the door then continued "I am glad to see they didn't lose complete control" while looking at Nora, Bita, and Ruka. They nodded and turned to the door as Ren and Fang walked in.

Yuki and Luna jumped in between Ren and William while I grabbed Kagome's arm because they started to run at him. Yuki said "he is a friend." William asked "if you are a friend, why did you try to abduct Haruna at my castle?" He said "because I wanted her to come home and not be in danger anymore, but you prevented it. I got rid of Yamato when he almost captured her. Before he could answer I said "William, you don't need to worry. He was worried about me because he is my brother whom I told you about." He said "He is? I thought you were older than him." I said "No, he is older than me by two minutes." He said "you are twins" with surprise.

I nodded, looked at Ren after everyone settled down and said "Now Ren, why did you come here? We would have seen you in the morning." He said "I need to tell you something." I said "What could you not wait to tell until morning?" He said "I am the one who brought Katara and the others here. It was the only way I thought I could get you back here since you lost your memory."

I asked "You didn't hurt them, did you? Where are they now?" He said "I put them to sleep and transported them to the abandoned shack on the cliff in the craggy swamp." I said "you put them there knowing you and I are the only ones able to go in it, not even Luna can go there." He said "exactly" then looked at William as he asked "Why are you two the only ones able to go there?" I said "because everyone who goes there gets swallowed by the swamp." He asked "Then how did he get them to the shack?" He answered "I am the only one who knows the true path and craggy swamp is one of my domains. The only reason Haruna can go in is because it knows she is the balance." He repeated "it knows" in a curious manner. I said "yes, the swamp is alive." He said "oh" as he looked down.

Ren said "We can go get them tomorrow. The main reason I came here was to get you guys for dinner." I nodded and went to eat dinner before heading to bed. While everyone was asleep, I started to walk to the swamp with Kiba right by my side. He refused to let me go alone. Since Kiba and Fang can go in as well I allowed him to come along.

I was surprised to see Ren and Fang waiting for us at the shack. He said "I knew you would wait for everyone to go to sleep before coming here." I said "Yes, I want them back. Why are you here?" He said "I knew you would forget I am the only one able to take anyone through." I said "I remembered but you had people following you."

He said "They were following you and are waiting for you to leave." I asked "Why are they after me?" H said "because they are Yamato's men." I said "Just great" with annoyance in my voice. He said "Calm down. I have a plan, but it involves you leaving alone, only for a short while" while looking at Kiba who is giving him a death stare.

CHAPTER 30

Ren got Katara and the others out of the swamp through the true path while I got out on my own at the opposite side. Once I left the swamp and got a little distance from it, someone confronted me. As I watched them closely, they said "Princess Haruna, you need to come with me." I said "I knew you were following me until the swamp, I am not going with you because you are from Yamato's group."

He said "You are smart for seeing through that, but you are still coming with us" with an evil grin while signaling the others. I said "you still won't take me with you" while catapulting myself over them and continued to run when I landed. They yelled "GET HER!!" and started running after me. I ran to the cliff Ren had told me to lure them to and pretended to be cornered. When they surrounded me, he said "Now you have nowhere to run. We have you surrounded."

I said "Oh no..... Whatever shall I do" sarcastically. He heard the sarcasm in my voice and said "you can't escape us." I gave them an evil look while laughing and said "Did you think I came alone?" and looked up. They followed my gaze and saw Ren and Fang above us while Kiba jumped down the cliff. When I got on his back, he started to run at them. Ren yelled "GO!!!!! We will handle them and catch up to you!" I looked behind me after we jumped over them, I watched as Ren continued to fight them. As I turned back to focus in front of me, I saw Ren send them to his abyss which no one can escape.

REN

I caught up to them on Fang and continued to go back to the palace while the sun rose in the sky. I said "I got all your friends back to mother and father. They are with William and the others waiting for us to return. I managed to get to my position right as you got there. Kiba insisted on following you at a safe distance until he got to his spot." She said "Thank you for the plan. It worked perfectly." I said "Yea it did" as we came into view of the palace.

HARUNA

I saw Katara and the others and raced to them. I said "I am sorry this happened but you are in my home world Murina." When I got to them, Katara said "It's ok, we didn't get hurt but who is the man who brought us here?" I said "He is my twin brother Ren. He thought bringing you here was the only way to get me back to Murina." She said "Oh... so you are not a resident of earth." I said "No, I am a princess of Murina and balance of it. I was chased to earth because my life was in danger." She gasped and said "Oh...." as she started to bow. I said "No, you don't need to bow. You are my friends, and I am going to get you back to earth." She nodded and looked at mother and father.

I looked at her as she said "So these are your friends from earth." I nodded as she smiled and said "There is something I have had on my mind." I asked "what is it?" She said "When you take your friends back to earth, I need you to bring Haru and Elie to me." I said "What?! but they are dead and have already been buried." She shook her head as she said "They aren't dead. Yamato knew a forbidden spell that pulls it's victims soul out of their body and makes it look like they are dead."

I said "What?! but they are probably rotted." She said "They are not, the spell keeps their bodies alive. I can reverse it if you bring me their bodies." I said "Ok, we will leave right away." I got to the portal while Ren and Luna stayed behind to wait for us to return. I looked at everyone and said "Stay calm and don't worry you will be home soon. Now go through the portal." They nodded and went through.

We landed in Katara's office at least what used to be her office. We were shocked to see both Alorrur and Burruna are in ruins. I looked around and immediately started running toward the two areas I put the barriers and found most of the villagers in the graveyard. Most of them yelled "Haruna! Someone was asking for your whereabouts. When we told her we didn't know where you were, she destroyed Alorrur and Burruna. The two places you put barriers around, the graveyard and your mansion, are unscathed. Everyone ran to these areas to avoid death.

I knew I had to put up the barriers but could not figure out why. It appears I am still being hunted" said I. Kyo walked up to me and said "It was a girl named Kagura who was hunting you. She wants revenge for the capture of Jiro and condemnation of Yamato." He saw the shocked and worried expression I gave him and immediately knew it was worse than he thought. I said "So she was strong enough to escape the guards and had enough power to destroy Alorrur and Burruna. I will deal with her myself. Have everyone stay in the barriers until I can fix the villages and hunt down Kagura." I looked at Haru and Elie's graves and continued "In the meantime I've got a mission to complete right now."

Everyone cleared a path for us and watched as I walked up to their graves. When I stopped in front of their tombstones, their souls manifested in front of me. Everyone gasped and backed away. I said "I got all my memories back. I met with mother and father, and they said they want me to bring your bodies back so mother can reverse the spell Yamato cast on you." Elie said "Thank goodness you guys are alright. When Kagura came and destroyed the villages, we thought she got you too. We are ready to return to Murina. Please take our bodies lady Haruna." They looked at Kiba and continued "We are glad you are back with lady Haruna." He said "same here, I am never leaving her side again."

Everyone asked "Did that cat just talk?" I said "Everyone don't be scared, they won't hurt you…. but they are not normal cats. They chose this form so they wouldn't scare you." Kyo said "They are your familiars, aren't they? They are probably bigger in their true forms." I said "Yes, now let's show them your true forms." Kiba said nodded and watched as Nora, Ruka, and Bita went into their true forms. Everyone gasped and were amazed, they looked at Kiba and asked "why didn't he transform back?"

I said "because he is more intimidating than others but if you want to see his true he will go back to it." they nodded and watched as he transformed. Kyo said" So they are sabertoothed tigers." "Yes, and they won't hurt you" said I. William looked at the position the sun was and said "We need to get Haru and Elie back to your mother so she can undo the spell. We can bring volunteers to help rebuild the villages after we finish our mission." I said "Ok, stay in the barriers until we come back." They nodded as we walked away. We got to the portal and went inside.

CHAPTER 31

When we landed in Murina we were surprised to see thirty palace guards waiting for us around the portal. I asked "Why were you waiting for us to return?" The captain of the knights, Kasuto, said queen Serina and king Raden said to accompany you home and to wait. Were you able to get them home? It is good to see Haru and Elie again but sad to see them in this state. It must have been hard on them." I said "yes and it is almost over. Mother will break the spell on them." I looked at the portal and continued "Kagura, one of Yamato's subordinates, destroyed Alorrur and Burruna, while we were away so we need to take volunteers to help repair the villages after we break the spell on Haru and Elie." He nodded and started escorting us to the palace.

We gave Haru and Elie to the palace healers and waited for mother and father to come and reverse the spell. Once she arrived, she said "now that their bodies are back on Murina, I can start to remove the spell. Once they are back to normal, they will have to be in the infirmary for about two weeks then they can return to their original duties." When Haru and Elie woke I was surprised to see they weren't phased at all. They only had to stay in the infirmary to get their bodies back to normal and rehydrate. They said "It was nice to be your parents even for the short time, but we must get to being your parents' bodyguards. It seems you have found very good replacements for us. Yuki and Kagome are perfect bodyguards for you and William for there is nothing else better than having a friend as a bodyguard." I said "yes, they have been there for William all his life and been there for me long before I met them. Now I have some villages to rebuild so I will get a couple hours of sleep and head back to earth.

WILLIAM

They said "ok, have a nice nap" and remained in the infirmary. I talked to Serina while Kiba went with Haruna while she takes her nap. I said "We are going to need volunteers to help us rebuild Alorrur and Burruna." She said "I am well aware of your needs. Kasuto informed me before I came to heal Haru and Elie. I am also sending some knights to protect you while you rebuild the villages." We went to the throne room and waited for Haruna to wake.

HARUNA

I was surprised to see Luna and Ren waiting for Kiba and I while standing on either side of them were Fang and Yuna. Ren said "Mother and father found volunteers to help rebuild and some knights to guard you while you build. They also want Luna and I to accompany and help you as well." I said "Ok, take me to them." He said "Right this way sis" and took me to the throne room.

When we got to the throne room mother said "We have thirty volunteers and twenty knights going with you along with Ren and Luna. There is also something we thought of....... Katara and everyone who know about Murina are allowed to come here to visit and the other way around as well." I said "Thank you mother, father. We are going to build the villages now." They said "be safe" as we walked out and I nodded "we will."

We went through the portal and landed in the school again. I said "let's get the school and station built first. I'll rebuild the school; you guys rebuild the station. They said "yes my lady" and started construction of the village. I then went to the room the portal is in and made the old office into a medium sized room at which can only be opened through Katara's new office and made a lock for the door and Katara will be the only human on earth with the key. I finished the rest of the school and put a unique security system from Murina in it. nothing will go on without my knowledge. If anything happens, I will know while Kasuto is watching it.

I found Katara and explained the security system to her and about the key to the portal room. I said "You are the only one on earth allowed to have the key. Only those who know about me and Murina may enter and visit the others and I. William, Luna, and I have the other keys." She said "That is an excellent idea and it will keep enemies from using your portal." I said "Exactly, now let's get the rest of Alorrur and Burruna rebuilt."

She nodded and watched as I built rows of houses, restaurants, and shops.

I waited for everyone to finish the parts and the horses' stables so we could work on the hospital. When we finished the hospital, we noticed everyone came out of the barriers and began to help us. The two villages became closer through this experience. It is funny how disasters always bring people together.

CHAPTER 32

We made inns so travelers could rest and let their horses rest in the stables if they have them. Kyo walked up to me when we finally finished rebuilding Alorrur and Burruna a month later and said "These two villages are well guarded and stronger than before. Queen Harushia assigned guards to the villages and around the high school knowing the portal is there. She knows Katara is the only one outside the royal families of Herodia and Yasamada who is allowed to have a key to the portal room. By the way does that mean I am allowed to visit too?" I said "Yes, it is nice of Harushia to do that and yes you can visit too. There will be a list of names on both sides of the portal so Katara and Kasuto will know who is allowed. I will also go between worlds."

He said nodded and started to walk to the station but stopped and continued "You know everyone in Alorrur and Burruna think of you as a hero." I said "Yes and I will continue to protect them" with a smile. Ren walked up to me and said "We should return to mother and father to report our success. We also need to get everyone home." I said "Ok, just let me say bye to everyone then get William and the others." He said "very well" and waited by the portal.

I explained to him "I am staying a couple more days here to make sure everyone is safe then go home." He agreed but frowned when Luna said "She was also staying with me and went through the portal with everyone else. I said "let's go home and sleep. We can help around the villages tomorrow." They nodded and went to the mansion, then went to sleep.

Before everyone woke, I went to the market with Kiba to get food for everyone. When we got back Kiba laid down in the doorway of the kitchen while I made breakfast for everyone. I just finished cooking when I saw Renji come running on with blood all over his hands and urged me outside. Kiba followed as he always does and immediately tensed up as a woman covered in blood and deep cuts is unconscious on the ground. I said "Kiba! run and get Kyo to come here now!" He said "Will do.... Just make sure you get her patched up enough to stop the bleeding before he comes" and ran off to get him.

Nora came out with Yuna while stopping Bita and Ruka from coming out behind them. Nora said "Haruna, I came when I smelled the blood. The others are still sleeping. We need to get her healed now because if she dies you will be devastated." I asked "Why would I be sad?" She said "You cannot tell from all the blood on her, but I know her scent and it is definitely her. She is Katara." I said "Oh no...." with a shocked expression "Wait.... who would hurt her this badly and why?" She said "I *don't know but you can ask her when she regains consciousness and is in better health."*

KIBA

I got to Kyo's house but he was not there, so I ran to the new fire station and found him there. Everyone got worried when they saw my true form charging at them. They started to come toward me with anything they could use as a weapon. Before they could do anything stupid with them, Kyo ran in front of them and said "Stop! He will not hurt you. He is Haruna's familiar. He is actually a sabertoothed tiger from her home planet." They said "Wait.... he is that little black cat who is always by her side. Why is he here in his true then?" He got worried when he heard them say that and said "If you never go far from Haruna, why are you here in your true form without her?" I said "because she sent me here. Katara was attacked and is barely breathing. She doesn't know it is Katara, but I know her scent. We need you to bring a medical kit immediately. I will take you to her mansion."

He said "Wait she has a mansion?" I said "Yes, she built it herself with the help of the Yarashias. She told me before she went to sleep last night. Now let's get you to your horse and go." He nodded and rushed to his horse and got the medical kit then followed me to the mansion.

HARUNA

I finally got the bleeding to stop when I saw Kyo on his horse beside Kiba coming this way. I said "We need to help her now. Nora told me this is Katara. Is that why you said to stop the bleeding?" When Kyo walked up to heal her, Kiba said "Yes and I knew she would tell you." I said "Yes, now we need to get her healed. I noticed Yuki was on the roof and said "You went with me to the market along with Kiba didn't you?" He said "Yes, Kiba and I never leave your side since he is your familiar and I am your bodyguard. He knew I was following you too. He kept looking back at me when you were walking in front of him."

I nodded and started to heal Katara's wounds. We heard her cough an hour later and went to her. She said "Sorry I followed you here so I could finally know where you live. When I started to go home, Kagura walked up to me and said 'tell me where Haruna is. I know she is back in the village.' When I refused, she attacked me. I do not know how I managed to escape her but I did. I managed to get to the guards here before passing out." I said "You are safe now and we healed you. All you need now is rest." She nodded and went to sleep.

I went outside and told Yuki "I need you to do something for me." He said "what?" "I need you to go to Mabari high and help the teachers while Katara is here. Don't worry if anything happens, I will get you" said I. He nodded and left. I went to search the area for Kagura with Kiba but found no sign of her. I went back to the mansion to tell everyone "We are going back to Murina. We will be back later so don't worry. I think Kagura went to Murina, so we need to give chase."

They said "understood" and got back to their posts. I went to Mabari high and set an assembly for everyone there. When everyone got to the courtyard I said "Everyone needs to listen to Katara and the teachers along with the students who stayed to help after graduating. If you don't listen to them, they will get me and believe me when I say you do not want to get me mad by not listening to them." When the assembly was done, I walked back to my mansion with Yuki and Kiba then did some work before I went to bed.

CHAPTER 33

I went to check the security systems in Alorrur and Burruna to see if they were working as good as the ones in Murina. They were, so I walked around for a while. Everyone kept saying they were happy to see us still protecting them. I remembered I still did not tell the students from the incident in Murina about what I told Katara, so I went to school and had Katara call the names of the students who were involved to the courtyard. When everyone arrived, we sealed the doors closed so no one except those within the courtyard could hear.

They asked "Why are we here? Are we in trouble?" I said "No, I just needed to tell you guys what is going on before I return to Murina. Everyone who is here right now knows about Murina due to the incident. We do not want anyone to tell anyone else unless it is a last resort. You guys are the only ones allowed to visit Murina to visit me or explore but you will have a guard assigned to you while you are there. They will wait for you to come back when you go home. They will not leave Murina. There is a list with the names of everyone here which allows passage. If anyone who's name is not on the list goes to Murina, a knight will bring them to me to evaluate them."

They asked "What will happen when you leave?" I said "Do not worry Katara is the only one on earth with the key to the room with the portal in it. Alorrur and Burruna will be fine because they have the best security system from Murina in them. If anything happens, I will know." They said "thanks" and were dismissed. I walked up to Katara and said "I have not given you the key yet so here" and handed it to her. We then went to the portal and were on our way to Murina.

CHAPTER 34

When we landed on Murina, we found ourselves surrounded by thirty knights. Kasuto walked up to me and got a little spooked because Luna made herself visible again. She had been so silent I forgotten she had stayed behind with us. He then said "queen Serina has ordered us to protect the portal and to have ten knights accompany you to Runeshia palace. I will stay here to guard the portal with the remaining knights. Lord Ren is fighting off the attackers." I said "let me guess, Kagura is leading them."

He said "Yes, how did you know?" I said "She is the one who destroyed the villages. She is looking for me." He said "So that is why she sent us. After lord Ren filled her in, she sent us here." I said "Guard the portal well. We are going to build a tower to house it and post a squad here with you leading it. I will explain everything later." He said "understood my lady" and stationed men around the perimeter.

We started to go to the palace and had to stop when we got to the middle of the jungle. We encountered Ren fighting alongside four knights against four enemies. We started to run to help but Ren saw us and yelled "NO, get to the castle now

Haruna! It is you and Luna they are after!" I yelled "I was already doing that! You had better come back unscathed." He yelled "I will .... now get going." I ran toward the palace but yelled "STOP" at the edge of the jungle.

I yelled "We were being followed the whole time we were running and are already surrounded." I started evading attacks until everyone was attacking someone. I went to help Luna who noticed was having trouble but out of nowhere two people appeared and knocked us out. I heard everyone yell "No!!!!" and saw Kiba and Yuna running toward us before I blacked out.

WILLIAM

I started to run toward them but could not make it because I had to deflect a sword coming down on my back. I yelled "Kiba, Yuna.... We will get them back. You two know their scent and can feel the connection between you two." Kiba said "Yea, we need to let Ren and Queen Serina know what happened. I will tell Ren, you guys tell Serina." I said "very well" and finished everyone off with my powers over the ground so we could make it to the palace.

KIBA

I talked to Fang telepathically, I can only do that with Fang and Nora, and said "Haruna and Luna were abducted, and we do not know where they were taken." She said "ok, I let Ren know. He said to go tell Serina. We will handle this." I said "already on it" and ran with Yuki staying alongside me.

WILLIAM

We got to the palace and said "Haruna and Luna have been abducted. We couldn't stop them in time. We will get them back because I love Haruna and plan to marry her one day." When Serina came in my room since she wanted my report alone, she said "We knew you were together. We also know you will protect her to the best of your abilities so we will definitely approve your marriage, but we need to get them back first." I said "I know and thank you" then followed her to the war room.

HARUNA

I woke in a camp surrounded by the desert sands. I am guessing we are in the Haranama desert because the color of the sand is a mix between gold and red. I looked across from where I am tied and noticed Luna is still unconscious. The guards saw I awoke and came to me. The commander of the guards who took us said "I see you have awoken. I am Hara, leader of this company." I said "I know why you need me but why Luna?"

He said "We need her because she is the key to the area, we need to take you. The planets core which dwells in a temple in the mountains which can only be accessed through this desert." I said with surprise "You know where the core is. I thought my family were the only ones who know where it's location is." He said "No, I have been searching secretly for master Yamato, but your brother sent him to his inescapable abyss. I will finish his work with Kagura by my side." I said "No you won't. I will never destroy Murina." He said "Yes, you will and we will keep you at the fort in this desert until it is time for us to fulfill our mission. Now go back to sleep" and knocked me out before I could say anything else.

CHAPTER 35

WILLIAM

We came to a conclusion a half hour later. We are going to follow Kiba and Yuna to them and take them back by force. We will then get rid of Kagura and whoever it was who took them. Kiba said "We are going to search for them now." I said "Ok Nora will let me know if you find them." He nodded and left with Yuna.

KIBA

I led Nora to a spot in the Haranama desert and said "This is where they were last. Their scent is gone. Apparently, whoever took them knew we would follow their scent here. We will have to follow our connection from here on. go and get the others and take them to this spot then follow our scent from here. Yuna and I will continue looking." She nodded and ran back the way we came.

I looked at Yuna and said "We will find them. Nothing can keep us from them." She said "I know now let's go. The sooner we find them the better." I nodded and continued to follow our link. We decided to wait when we found an abandoned fort so we could see what they were planning. I said "If they are planning what I think they are, I will kill them and won't give Ren a chance to send them to his abyss." Fang walked beside me and said "You don't have a choice. He is already inside." I asked "how long?" She said "Ten minutes...... He has a connection with Haruna too remember."

I said "Yes because he is her twin. There is no doubt he will find her. They can feel each other's pain." She said "Not only that. He is the true key to the core. He keeps her in check and Haruna is the core, that is why she is known as the 'balance'." I said "What? I thought Luna was the key and I knew Haruna is the core but very few people know what being the balance actually means." She said "No, Ren and Haruna agreed to let Luna pose as the key so if something like this ever happened, they would never have both the key and the core. Now stay here until he gives us the signal to help." I said "very well" and began to wait.

Ren came out with two people and said "They are not here. I managed to put Hara in the abyss. The others were taken to lord Hamaria's castle dungeon. They rescued Haruna and Luna and took them to the castle. They are his guests until we come and get them, but we need to wait for the others before we go so let's wait here." I said nodded and continued waiting.

HARUNA

I woke to a guard sitting in a chair beside the bed I am laying in. She said "It is ok, you are in lord Hamaria's castle. We caught wind of you and lady Luna being abducted. We knew where they would have taken you, so we went to assault it. You two were still unconscious when we got to you, so we brought you here. Lady Luna is in the next room. Lord Hamaria would like you to change into one of the dresses and come to the dining room. Lady Luna has already eaten and is resting in her bed.

I said "I know I should thank him but I would rather stay in this room until the others come and get us." I heard a voice from the corner of the room say "You should eat even a sacred being as powerful as you need to eat. Especially when you look as famished as you do right now. I want you to change because I need to wash your clothes and get the sand off them before the others arrive, besides you look more like a warrior than a princess so you should dress like one even if it is just a couple hours."

I said "very well but only for a couple hours" and went to the dining room after I changed. While I ate I asked "How did you hear about us being kidnapped?" He said "I have had spies watching you since you first came back to Murina. I have wanted to help you and was trying to find a way to get you back to Murina, but Ren beat us to it."

I said "So if Ren hadn't done what he did, you would have found a way to get me back here. Why are you so fascinated in us?" He said "I have been a guardian to you, Ren, and Luna since you were born so why wouldn't I want to protect you." I said "Just because you are our uncle doesn't make you our guardian." He said "Yes it does, lets finish eating and get your clothes cleaned." I said "fine" and walked around the palace until my clothes were washed.

I was walking in the courtyard with Luna a couple hours later when a maid walked up to us and said "Here are your clothes. Follow me to your rooms to change into them." We walked to Luna's room and decided to change there. We walked back to the courtyard after thanking the maid and continued our walk.

We started to walk to the library to read while we waited for the others but was jumped from behind. The guards started running for us but were also jumped. I grabbed my sword and blocked hits meant for Luna and fended off our attackers. We went to help the guards but were too late. They were already killed and their killers were running at us. I said "we need to get out of here now" after I killed the assailants and more started running at us.

We got to the front of the throne room and found Narme fending off attackers. We ran to him, but he yelled "NO! Get out of here! It's you two they are after!" I said "You better survive this uncle Narme because if you don't you will never be our protector." He said "Don't worry I'll survive. It's my knights and you two I'm worried about...... Now Go!"

CHAPTER 36

We fought our way to the front of the castle when we were suddenly surrounded. They were closing in on us when Kiba and Yuna jumped over them, told us to get on their backs, and jumped back over them when we were on their backs. Once we were clear of the assailants Ren and his troops came out of the forest and rushed the castle.

William ran up to us on Nora's back and said "You are safe. When we were walking through the forest to come get you, we noticed troops and waited for them to strike. Turns out Kagura has some of the nobles on her side. We need to put a stop to this." I said "I was thinking the same thing" and waited for Yuki and Kagome to be signaled to us. Yuki said "I am never leaving your side again." I said "I know" and watched Ren kill the attackers, send his army into the castle, and run over to us.

He said "We need to get you out of here." I said "We need to help lord Hamaria." He said "We need to get you out of here first." I got frustrated and said "fine" then started to follow him. William came up beside me and said "I know this isn't a good time to ask but things keep happening, so I have no choice but to ask now. Will you marry me?" I said "Yes but right now we need to help lord Hamaria." He said "That makes me happy to hear that and I agree" while smiling at me. I smiled back then looked toward Ren and yelled "We shouldn't leave our uncle to fend for himself. We need to reveal what we are. I am tired of running!" He said "very well, if that is what you truly want" and turned back toward the castle. We were surrounded once we reached the gate and were pleased to see Kagura finally reveal herself. She said "you and Luna are going to destroy this world whether you want to or not."

I said "let's see what Murina has to say about that. We got off Kiba and Fang then put our hands on the ground. The animals from all over Murina started to come and attack them. They left our allies alone and only attacked Kagura's troops. They started to retreat into the forest but were scooped up and thrown by the trees. She looked around in shock of everything crumbling before her.

She said "What is going on? Luna isn't doing anything....... It is only you and Ren." We smirked as Luna walked up to her and said "I was never the key, I only pretended to be so there would always be one of them safe and they don't heal or kill Murina. They can ask Murina for help. It is a power only they have and have always hidden until now."

She said "That can't be true.... We never sensed the power of the key in Ren. We only sensed it in you and how could you be friends with the planet itself?" I walked up to her after Luna looked at me and said "It is an ability we have since we are the protectors of Murina. We can communicate with her. Ren has an ability to hide his aura and send it onto someone else. He did it to Luna after she agreed to be his substitute.

Luna said "I will do anything if it means protecting my older brother and sister, even if it means becoming their decoy. Ren said "It is time we put an end to this and defend Murina." Kagura laughed and said "do you really think this will end with my death.... There will always be someone coming after you for your powers. There is one more thing I have to say, how would you feel if we killed Katara and everyone in Alorrur and Burruna?"

She laughed as I lunged toward her sword in hand and grabbed my sword cutting her palm as the blade dug into her skin. As blood dripped down her arm from her hand she said "We will have you and Ren one way or another. We know you, Ren, and Luna are immortal. We don't know what Luna's purpose is yet, but we will find out soon enough." I laughed and said "you don't understand, every sacred being with a sabertoothed tiger as a familiar is immortal." She got a shocked expression as she manipulated the wind and called to her men "RETREAT" then vanished from view.

CHAPTER 37

REN

I said "We need to check on my soldiers and uncle Narme."
Haruna agreed and went with Yuki and I to see if he is ok
while William and Kagome watched the perimeter. We got to
uncle Narme's bodyguards and found out he is perfectly fine. He
killed all his attackers and was sitting on a chair in his study
and reading up on Kagura. He said "Oh no..... you guys need
to get to Alorrur and Burruna and put everyone on guard to
protect everyone there." Haruna asked "why?" with a worried
look. He said "because she never goes back on her word."

HARUNA

Ren looked at me and asked "what's your hurry? She didn't
promise us anything." I said "yes she did. Right before she
vanished, she said she is going to kill Katara and everyone in
Alorrur and Burruna. When I looked at her, I knew she meant
it because the look in her eyes. We need to warn and protect
them now" then ran to the courtyard with Ren and the others
behind me.

I filled everyone in on the situation as we made our way to the portal and sent Kiba to inform mother and father on what's happening. They sent a company of guards with us to defend the villages while I protected the school from Kagura. I said "We need to split up and patrol the area. It will be easier to protect everyone that way." Yuki stayed with me while Luna and Ren paired off and William and Kagome went to patrol Alorrur.

We sounded the emergency alarm system we recently installed and started to tell the villagers to stay indoors until further notice. Katara ran up to me and asked "what is happening? Did you manage to stop Kagura?" I said "Sorry, we stopped her from catching us but she said she would kill you and destroy Alorrur and Burruna to get to Ren and I. We will stop her before anything happens." She said "oh no..." smiled after a few minutes "I have complete faith in you. You will protect us, you always do."

I said "Thank you" and started to draw my sword because Kagura appeared directly behind Katara. I yelled "I am not going to make it!" as I ran toward Kagura. Before she could kill Katara, Kiba ran, got her on his back, and got her away as I made contact with her sword. Yuki ran up to me to help but I said "don't worry about me. I will deal with Kagura.... I need you to go check on Katara. If she isn't hurt tell Kiba to protect her and have Bita help them then come and help me." He nodded and ran to her then came back to help but got jumped by two of Kagura's lieutenants.

Kagura yelled "Don't look away from your opponent. You will only get stabbed in the back when you do!" as I blocked her strike. I said "You won't be able to stab me in the back that easily." The fighting is still going and it has been five hours *since it began. It is still a stale mate between Kagura and I but sooner or later one of us is going to fall and hopefully it won't be me. Yuki keeps getting jumped. It seems she brought her whole army to make one last grandstand against us.*

REN

Seven hours have past and Alorrur and Burruna have become a massive graveyard and battleground. We keep protecting the villagers but there is still no sign of Haruna, Katara, and Yuki. I ran into William, literally bumped into him, while searching for missing villagers. I said "You need to get your mother to help us. We keep trying to get to Haruna but keep getting jumped by soldiers. We need her help. Haruna is still fighting Kagura and is starting to weaken. If we don't get to her soon, they will have her then they will turn their attention on me." He said "Wait.... she is still fighting Kagura. How long?" I said "Since the attack first started. Please go and get reinforcements from your mother and father."

WILLIAM

I said "Ok I'll go with Kagome and get mother and father to send reinforcements. Just work on holding off the assault and keep trying to get to Haruna." He said "You don't have to tell me because I am already doing just that" as Kagome and I got on Ruka and Nora. We began to run to the palace but noticed the army is already halfway to the villages. We continued to run toward them and noticed they think we are the enemy. We slowed down when we heard mother yell "Stand down! It is William and Kagome!" They stopped and waited for mother's instructions. She rode up to us and said "It is good you found Ruka and Nora. Does this mean Haruna went back to Murina?" I said "Yes and no..... Katara and everyone at Marabi high were taken to Murina by her brother Ren to lure her back to Murina. When we got to Murina, Kiba unsealed her memories and helped her fend off Kagura after we got everyone back and repaired the villages but now Kagura is attacking the villages again and we can't get to Haruna. Every time we try to get to her we get jumped."

Mother said "We know she is in danger. That is why we are on our way to help right now. You two can lead us to her so we can save her.

REN

We got to Haruna's mansion to get her guards to help get her. Renji said "I will help you while the others help the villagers." I said "Ok let's go" and went to her but was attacked again. I looked over at Haruna when we finally managed to get close enough to see her and are shocked to see the state she is in. I felt her pain but didn't think she is so badly injured.

HARUNA

I continued to try to dodge her to no avail. I have deep gashes all over my body and can barely stand. I am surprised to see her stop and say "You know, you probably do not know this but when you get severely injured as you are right now, you always lose control of yourself and start attacking friend and foe alike. My plan has never been for me to kill Katara. It has been for you to lose control and kill her yourself."

I looked at her with an angered look and said "Why do you think I would attack friends?" She said "because you did it before on Murina, but your brother calmed you down. After that they tried to make sure you never got injured to that extent again, but I am about to make their darkest fear come true." I asked "How could you possibly know about that?" She said "because we were watching you that day as well in secret of course. We watched as you killed your uncle Narme when he was visiting you on your third birthday while your little sister Luna was beside you. It is because of her your uncle was brought back and became your guardian. It is because she is your and Ren's guardian. She still looks like a fourteen-year-old girl because she fully awakened when she was fourteen. You and Ren fully awakened when you were eighteen, William when he was nineteen, and Yuki and Kagome when they were twenty-one."

I remembered the pain and shock on everyone's faces as they watched me attack and kill uncle Narme. Ren was the only one who could match my skill and calm me down and since Luna is our guardian, she brought him back to life but at the cost of him becoming Luna's subordinate and our second guardian. As I was still lost in my memory, Kagura swung her sword toward my head. I went to deflect it with my sword but she changed directions at the last second and sliced my arm clear down to the bone. I lost control the moment her sword left my arm.

CHAPTER 38

REN

I watched in horror as I watched Kagura slice Haruna's arm and saw her eyes turn blood red as her sword left her arm, after I killed the soldiers attacking me, I started to have a flash back of the first time we learned Haruna loses control when she gets severely injured then said "Oh no..... It's happening all over again." Renji was about to say something but stopped as Kagura yelled "YES!!!!! I finally managed to get her to lose control! Now to get her to kill Katara!"

I yelled "You Fool!!! No one can control her when she loses control. She attacks whoever catches her attention!" William arrived at the worst possible time with reinforcements. When he saw how badly she was injured he started to run toward her. I yelled "Don't take another step toward her!!!! She has lost control and will attack anyone who catches her attention!" My warning came too late because the moment he said "What?" with a shocked expression, she lunged at him. He tried to dodge her but was kicked in the stomach and flung across the school yard. Nora caught and put him on the ground while Luna and

Yuna ran and put a healing barrier around them. The wind and sound of impact echoed through the village as I yelled "Everyone stay away from her while I try to calm her down!" While running to intercept her next attack on William.

Katara asked "can't she hurt you too?" I said "I am the only one who can match her skill and strength when she loses control and calm her down." She said "Ok, be careful" and watched as I made contact with her next attack. The same attack that knocked William out didn't faze me one bit, and I began to continuously fend off her attacks. It took an agonizing two hours to weaken her so Kiba could tackle her so I could calm her down. I immediately sent my aura into her to calm her down.

HARUNA

When I came to I asked "What happened?" Why is Kiba on top of me and why are both of you sad?" as Kiba got off and laid down beside me, Ren said "You lost control again and I had to calm you down before you could do anymore damage to William. Luna is tending to him right now."

I said "I know I lost control again. Thank you for calming me down....... Wait, did you say I hurt William?" He said "yes" still looking sad. Tears started to fall down my cheeks as I said "How? He was not around when I lost control." He said "He arrived with reinforcements and saw how badly you are injured and started to run to you shortly after you lost control. You must have lost consciousness this time as well." I said "yes, I will go check on him. Are you going to stop the rest of the army?" He said "yes, now go. Luna put up a healing barrier around him so you should step into it so you can start to heal too." I nodded as Kiba showed me where they were.

I said after he regained consciousness and I got healed up a bit from the barrier "I'm sorry.... I didn't know I hurt you until Ren told me." He said "it's ok, you weren't yourself. I saw it in your eyes. They didn't have the normal glow in them when they turned red. Now don't worry about me. Luna is healing me. I may have a scar from this but at least I will live. Go help Ren and the others disperse the army and capture Kagura and finally end this mess once and for all." I nodded and went to help. Two hours later, we got everyone and everything settled down, defeated the army, and sent Kagura to the abyss.

When I got back to William, he was all healed up and said "So..... do you finally want to have our wedding?" I said "Yes, let's have it at Runeshia palace. Everyone in our families and our friends who know about Murina can come." A couple days later we finally got married with everyone close to us attending. Three days later after getting tired of doing the same routine, We made a pact to protect Murina and the two villages of Alorrur and Burruna and let's not forget Romora from now until the end of time.

Printed in the United States
by Baker & Taylor Publisher Services